Also by Ronald Kidd

Monkey Town: The Summer of the Scopes Trial

RONALD KIDD

Simon & Schuster Books for Young Readers
New York London Toronto Sydney

SIMON & SCHUSTER BOOKS FOR YOUNG READERS
An imprint of Simon & Schuster Children's Publishing Division
1230 Avenue of the Americas, New York, New York 10020
SIMON & SCHUSTER BOOKS FOR YOUNG READERS is a trademark of Simon & Schuster, Inc.
Book design by Chloë Foglia
The text for this book is set in Sabon.
Manufactured in the United States of America
2 4 6 8 10 9 7 5 3 1
Library of Congress Cataloging-in-Publication Data
Kidd, Ronald.
On Beale Street / Ronald Kidd.—1st ed.
p. cm.
Summary: In Memphis, in the 1950s, when fifteen-year-old Johnny Ross is introduced to
the blues, he ventures to the infamous Beale Street and finds
friendship with an up-and-coming young musician named Elvis Presley.
ISBN-13: 978-1-4169-3387-8 (hardcover)
ISBN-10: 1-4169-3387-5 (hardcover)
[1. Blues (Music)—Fiction. 2. Race relations—Fiction.
3. Segregation—Fiction. 4. Presley, Elvis, 1935–1977—Fiction.
5. Memphis (Tenn.)—Fiction.] I. Title.
PZ7.K5315On 2008
[Fic]—dc22
2007022583

In memory of my father, Paul Kidd

CONTENTS

PART 1

Folks, I've just been down, down to Memphis town
That's where people smile, smile on you all the while
They had a fellow there named Handy
  with a band you should hear
And while the dancers gently swayed, all the band boys
  played
Real harmony
I never will forget the tune
  that Handy called the Memphis Blues
Oh, them blues

—George A. Norton and W. C. Handy

CHAPTER ONE

It was a good day at Poplar Tunes.

I was a regular there, a fifteen-year-old kid in blue jeans who showed up on summer afternoons and combed the record bins, looking for the latest hits by Hank Thompson and Kitty Wells. Mr. Novarese, the owner, would set aside records he thought I might like. He was behind the counter when I walked in that day.

"Hey, Johnny, I got one for you," he called. "It's the new Eddy Arnold."

Reaching into my pocket, I pulled out a few coins and a crumpled-up dollar bill, all the money I had in the world.

"Thanks, Mr. Novarese," I said, "but I'll be looking in the used bins today."

Poplar Tunes was the best record store in Memphis and was an easy bus ride from my house. There were rows of bins, with every kind of music from country to pop. My favorite part was the used section, where you could pick up good records that had just a scratch or two.

As I started across the store, I noticed a familiar face. It was Ruth Ann Morris, who had been in my English class the year before. I had spoken to her once or twice but wasn't sure she even knew my name. I knew hers. Ruth Ann had a smile that made my throat tighten, and she seemed to float a few inches off the ground. She was wearing a plain skirt and blouse, but to me she looked like royalty.

I was working up the nerve to say something, when my foot caught on one of the bins and I went sprawling in the aisle. I looked up and saw Ruth Ann gazing down at me. She smiled, but it wasn't mean. It was cool and beautiful, like always.

"You were in my English class," she said. "Aren't you Johnny Ross?"

I nodded. "You're Ruth Ann Morris."

Scrambling to my feet, I bumped my head on the bin. I lurched back a step. She stood on her tiptoes and reached for the bump on my head. My skin tingled where she touched it.

"Does it hurt?" she asked.

"Not now," I said. I blushed, and she smiled again.

"What happened?" said a voice behind me. It was Mr. Novarese.

"I bumped my head. It's okay."

"Let me see," he said.

Sighing, I tilted my head so he could look. He crouched down and examined the record bin.

"Seems fine," he said.

Ruth Ann stifled a giggle, then asked him, "Can you

help me find a record? It's for my father's birthday."

"Johnny can help you," said Mr. Novarese. "He may have a hard head, but he knows his music."

He went back to the counter, while I helped Ruth Ann check the bins. We looked at country records first, then moved to male vocalists. Her eyes lit up when she saw "Oh! My Papa," a new record by Eddie Fisher.

"That's perfect!" she said.

Mr. Novarese rang up the record and put it in a bag. Ruth Ann started for the door, then hesitated.

"Thank you, Johnny," she said. She smiled. Then she was gone.

I spent more time looking through the bins, but my mind was still on Ruth Ann. I remembered her smile and the way she had touched me. Finally I picked out a couple of records and headed home.

"Hello, Memphis! Bob Neal here, frying eggs on the sidewalk and bringing you the top country hits. That was a new one from Webb Pierce."

I sat on our front steps, drinking an Orange Crush and listening to music. Sometimes on hot days I would bring the radio out onto our porch, trying to get away from the heat inside. A few people in the neighborhood had air-conditioning, but we didn't. Arthur Chapman did. He was my mother's boss. He owned half of downtown Memphis. Mr. Chapman had one of the biggest houses in town, and my mother and I lived in a cottage at the back of his property.

Bob Neal talked about Goody's Headache Powder, then

played more music. As I listened, a young man came around the corner of our house. He was a few years older than me, with skin the color of caramel. He glanced around, as if sizing the place up.

"What are you doing?" I asked.

I half expected him to run. Instead, he looked up at me. "You live here?"

"I said, what are you doing?"

"I'm supposed to trim your bushes," he said. "But if you live here, seems like you should do it."

"Where's Will?" I asked. Will was a combination gardener, handyman, and driver for Arthur Chapman.

The young man said, "Will's in the garage, working on the cars."

"Maybe I'll go get him."

"You do that," he said.

I stared at him, and he stared back.

He said, "Who are you?"

"Johnny Ross."

He nodded, then disappeared around the corner and came back holding a pair of gardening shears. He held them out to me. "You'll need these."

I didn't move. He shrugged. "Can't say I didn't try."

He turned to the bush. Holding the shears with a left-handed grip, he clipped off a few small branches.

"You're new," I said.

"Score one for the white boy."

"You talk different. Not just your accent."

He shook his head. "People in Memphis, they don't know what real Negroes sound like. We have opinions. We know what we want. We don't smile and shuffle."

He lowered the shears and held out his hand. "I'm Lamont Turner. From Chicago."

I shook his hand. I didn't know what else to do. Then I thought of something. "Turner? Are you any relation to Will?"

"Score two for the white boy. He's my father."

"I didn't know Will had a son."

"Now you do," he said.

"How did you get here?" I asked.

"Drove."

"You know what I mean."

He said, "Will Turner used to be married to my mother. They split after I was born, and we moved to Chicago. That's where I was raised. Early this year my mother was out of work. She has relatives in Memphis, and they got her a job, if you can call it that. A few weeks ago we moved back here."

"What's the job?" I asked.

"She's a maid. I bet you're impressed. Mother's a maid, father's a grunt."

"What about you?"

"I just finished high school," he said. "My father got me this job. Assistant grunt. This is my first day."

"You don't sound too happy about it."

"I'm happy about the money."

Money. It was something I thought about a lot. I guess that's the way it is when you don't have much of it. I thought about it now—how it would feel in my hand, what I would buy with it.

"Maybe I should get a job," I said.

"You *want* a job? Man, what's wrong with you? You got the American dream—no school, no work, just summer stretching out all day long."

"And night," I said. "I like it at night."

He smiled, looking someplace I couldn't see. "You like the nighttime, try the south side of Chicago. People on the streets. Laughing, drinking. Listening to music. I used to drive down there every chance I got."

I said, "You have a car?"

"Thirty-eight Ford. I'll take you for a ride sometime."

I hesitated. He saw it in my face.

"What's wrong, you scared? White boy don't want to be seen with a Nee-gro?"

Someone called, "Hey, Johnny!"

I looked around and saw Trey Chapman, Mr. Chapman's son. He was eighteen, with blond hair, big shoulders, and a bigger grin. Trey had just graduated from a fancy boarding school. Now that he was back home, he liked to drive through town in his Cadillac convertible. Sometimes he would hang around the house, trying to stir things up.

When Trey got closer, he shot me a smile that wasn't a smile. "What are you doing? Hanging out with the help?"

"I guess so," I said.

Trey turned to Lamont. "What are you staring at?"

"You," said Lamont.

Trey stepped toward him, so their noses were almost touching. Lamont didn't budge.

"This ain't Chicago," said Trey. "It's Memphis."

"So?" said Lamont.

Trey said, "You don't understand how it works around here."

"Maybe you could explain."

"This is how it works," said Trey.

He gave Lamont a hard shove. Lamont staggered back and fell to the ground. Dropping the gardening shears, he jumped to his feet, face flushed. He took a step toward Trey.

Trey grinned. "One more step and you're fired. Your father's fired. Your mother, too. Do it, man. Come on, take a step."

Lamont leaned forward, his hands working.

Trey said, "Or you could go for the jackpot. Hit me. Imagine how that would feel. Just one swing. You can do it, I know you can."

Lamont clenched his fists. Sweat dripped from his chin.

"Touch me," said Trey, "and your life's over."

Lamont reached for him. Trey's grin slipped, just for a moment. Then Lamont stopped, and Trey's grin came back.

Lamont said, "Another time, another place. I'll get you."

"You watch it, boy," said Trey.

Lamont gazed at him. Then, straightening his shoulders, he picked up the gardening shears and headed off.

Trey called after him. "Hey!"

Lamont turned around.

"Welcome to Memphis," said Trey.

He watched Lamont leave, then took a pack of cigarettes

from his pocket, shook one out, and lit it. Squinting through the smoke, he reached down and adjusted the dial on my radio. There was static, then the voice of Patti Page, singing a pop tune.

"You like that music?" I asked.

"Naw," he said. "But leave it on that station. WHBQ, at 560. Tonight at ten o'clock, Dewey Phillips comes on. He's got a show called *Red Hot and Blue*."

"You mean, like the flag?"

"No, man. *Red* Hot *and Blue*. Blue as in the blues. B. B. King. Big Mama Thornton. Rufus Thomas. Don't tell me you've never heard of them."

I shrugged.

Trey lowered his voice and looked around. "They're Negroes. They have their own kind of music. It's incredible."

"I thought you didn't like Negroes," I said.

"I love Negroes. Can't you tell? Anyway, I'm not planning to invite one home. I just like their music."

I said, "Is Dewey Phillips a Negro?"

Trey laughed. "A Negro? He's as white as you or me. But not normal white. He's loud white. Jumping white. Crazy white."

Trey took a long pull from his cigarette, then crushed it out on the porch next to me.

"Just listen tonight," he said. "You'll see."

He shot me a grin, then moved off across the yard.

That night I watched my mother make cornbread and black-eyed peas. She was tall, with wavy brown hair, dark eyes, and a forehead with a permanent set of wrinkles.

She had put an apron on over her business suit. As she moved around the kitchen, I could tell that her mind was still downtown, at work. She brought our food to the kitchen table and asked distractedly, "How was your day?"

I didn't say anything about Ruth Ann or Trey. I did tell her about Poplar Tunes, and I mentioned Will's son.

She looked up at me, her attention suddenly riveted. "Will's son?"

"Lamont. He's from Chicago."

I told her what he was like and how he had come to Memphis. I was surprised to realize that she already seemed to know about him.

She shook her head, worried. "Stay away from that boy."

"From Lamont? Why?"

"Just do as I say."

I dug in to the cornbread. She took a sip of coffee, eyeing me thoughtfully.

"I heard you come in last night," she said. "You were out late again, weren't you?"

"Aw, Mom."

For as long as I could remember, my mother had fallen asleep early, tired from work. I'd gotten into the habit of going out while she slept. Most of the time she didn't even know it.

"I don't like you running around at night," she said. "It's dangerous."

"I'm not little anymore. I'm fifteen."

"What do you do out there?" she asked.

"Nothing."

"You're going to get in trouble. I don't want to be woken up some night by the police."

"Thanks for the vote of confidence," I said.

"I mean it, Johnny. Find something else to do. Take up a hobby."

I remembered my conversation with Lamont. "Maybe I should get a job."

"A job?"

"We could use the money."

"That's crazy. You're a boy. It's summer. You're supposed to be having fun. Besides, I've got a perfectly good job."

"He hardly pays you anything," I said. "How long have you been with him? Twenty years? You practically run the place."

"Mr. Chapman's been good to us. He lets us stay in this house."

"And isn't it great," I said.

"What's that supposed to mean?"

"Come on, Mom. What are we doing here? This is the richest neighborhood in town. We don't have money. We don't have a big house. We don't belong. It's a pretend life. The kids at school know it. They laugh at me."

"Don't pay any attention to them."

"Wake up, Mom. You're dreaming. I'm not Trey Chapman. I never will be. At least let me make some money. Even Lamont has money."

She set her jaw and went back to eating. Shaking my head, I got up from the table and took my dishes to the sink, then went into my room and closed the door.

When I came out later she had fallen asleep on the sofa. I covered her with a quilt and went back to my room. Sitting on the bed, I turned on the radio and adjusted the dial to 560. A voice came flying out.

"Deegaw! Dewey Phillips comin' at you, just flat fixin' to bring you the hottest thing in the country, Red Hot and Blue, on WHBQ in Memphis, Tennessee. Wake up out there, just get ready. We're gonna play the first record for Denice, for Percy, for J. V., for Bernice, for Beulah, for Effie, for Oliver. We're gonna flat "Dig that Boogie" by Piano Red. Aw, just set on it, Red. If you can't set on it, lay on it."

Somebody started pounding on a piano and singing, *"Let's dig that boogie, let's dig that boogie."*

Dewey Phillips talked over the music, laughing, singing along. The music ended, and he kept on going.

"The next portion of Red Hot and Blue *comes to you courtesy of Lansky Brothers Clothing, down on Beale Street. They got easy credit. Just pay for it while you're wearin' it out. Go on and get you a wheelbarrow full of horseshoes and run 'em right through the front door. Just kick it down and tell 'em Dewey Phillips sent you. Yes sir, Lansky's. Down on Beale Street, where there's music every night. We got Piano Red at the Club House, Little Laura Dukes at*

*the Midway, Rosco Gordon at Pee Wee's Saloon.
Hey, Rosco, you there? Come on in, baby. No more
doggin'. You tell 'em."*

As he talked, a laid-back shuffling tune started, with a
saxophone and a singer whose voice was soft and hoarse:
"*No more doggin', foolin' around with you.*"

The music played. Dewey Phillips talked. There was
more music and more talking. Through it all I sat on my
bed, not moving.

There was something about that voice, that music. I'd
never heard anything like it. Half the time I couldn't
understand the words, but it didn't matter. It was pure feeling. It was life, spilling out of the speaker and into my
house. There were people out there, like the ones who
worked in mansions up and down the street, like Will, like
Lamont.

It was a place. It was a world—in the air, in my mind.
And it had a name. Beale Street. Beale Street, where there's
music every night.

I had always heard about Beale Street. I'd been there a
few times on my way to someplace else. It was downtown
for Negroes. They had their own stores, restaurants, the-
aters. It was right next to the white downtown, but it
could have been miles away. We had our world and they
had theirs, close by, related, parallel but never touching.
There was black. There was white. But there was never
gray. That's just the way it was in Memphis.

I thought about Beale Street, about the music and the
people. I wondered what it was like after dark.

CHAPTER TWO

If you're fifteen and like to get around, you learn to take the bus. That's where I was the following night, rumbling along Union Avenue toward downtown Memphis.

Earlier that evening my mother had worked on her ledger books for a while. By nine o'clock she was in bed, asleep.

I had taken some money from my dresser and checked the bus schedule, then headed out the door. Arthur Chapman's house was a few miles east of downtown on Belvedere Boulevard, a wide, parklike street lined with mansions.

I hurried up Belvedere toward Union Avenue. I was wearing a short-sleeved shirt, but because of the heat wave the temperature was still over ninety, and by the time I reached Union I was sweating. The bus came a few minutes later, and now here I was, on a trip to a place I'd heard about on the radio.

There were maybe ten other people on the bus, all of them Negro, all of them sitting at the back. That's the way it was in Memphis—whites in front, Negroes in back.

I got off the bus at Second and Union, downtown. I turned south, toward Beale Street.

As I walked, I heard music in my head, with Dewey Phillips shouting over it. The music continued, and then I realized it wasn't in my head anymore. It was in the air, faint but distinct, swirling like cigarette smoke. I heard other sounds in the distance. People were talking and laughing. Someone shouted. Glass broke.

I crossed Gayoso Street and started to see people. An old man sat on the curb. A woman walked toward me carrying a bottle, weaving from side to side. A couple came along behind her, arms wrapped around each other. The man saw me, said something to his friend, and they laughed. There were lots of people now. I looked around and realized I was the only white person in sight. I hesitated for a minute. Then I heard the music and started forward again.

I turned a corner, and suddenly I was there. Beale Street stretched in front of me, lit up by streetlights and neon. It was ten o'clock at night, but judging from the crowd you would have thought it was noon. The sidewalks were filled with people walking, talking, listening to music, and passing the time.

Next to one of the buildings, a man was sitting on a wooden stool, singing and playing a guitar. He told about a woman who had left him and run off with another man. The song was sad, but somehow it was funny at the same time. I wondered how that could be. The answer was somewhere in the man's face, among the wrinkles and scars, in the eyes, under the smile.

Nearby, a white police officer leaned against a corner of the building, chatting with a group of men and listening to the music. He saw me and frowned. Excusing himself, he came over. He cocked his head and looked down at me.

"Son, what do you think you're doing here?"

I shrugged. "Listening to the music."

"This is no place for you," he said. "Get on home now, you hear? When you wake up tomorrow, mow a lawn. Climb a tree. But don't come to Beale Street."

He stood there, waiting. I took one last look at the singer and moved off. I turned a corner and headed back the way I came. When I was sure the officer couldn't see me anymore I ducked into an alley, intending to double back around to Beale Street a block farther up. The alley was dark. As I moved along, a hand reached out and grabbed my arm. In the shadows I saw a man's face and smelled alcohol.

"Got some money, boy?"

"Uh, no," I said. My heart was pounding. I thought about the wallet in my back pocket.

"I think you do," the man said.

When he reached out, I twisted free of his grip and raced up the alley. A minute later I was back on Beale Street. I patted my back pocket to make sure the wallet was still there, then took a deep breath and kept walking.

I recognized a few stores and buildings from when I'd passed through the area during the daytime. There was the

Morris Pinstein Company, a ladies' shoe store. There was a pawn shop called Harry's Loans, where people could trade watches and jewelry for cash. There was the Avalon Pool Room and Buffington Tailors and the Blue Light Studio, where you could get four photos for a quarter.

There was Schwab's Drugs, which I was amazed to see was open for business. I wandered inside. The place didn't look like any drugstore I'd seen. It was a big, open room that had tables stacked with every kind of thing you could imagine, and a few you couldn't. There were dolls and birdhouses and something that looked like a fire hydrant. There were perfumes called Jickey Jockey and Lodestone. There was regular medicine, like aspirin and cough syrup, but there was also a section of homemade cures with names like Uncrossing Oil and John the Conqueror Root.

When I went back outside, the street was busier. I found myself swept along in a crowd of people, and I decided to see where they were going. It turned out to be the Palace Theater, a big building with movie posters in front, along with signs advertising live performers: W. C. Handy, Ella Fitzgerald, Louis Armstrong. On the marquee were the words AMATEUR NIGHT. I bought a ticket and went inside. The seats were full, but I found a place to stand against the back wall. A minute later the lights went down, and a voice rang out.

"It's amateur night on Beale Street!"

A short, chunky man stood on the stage, wearing a bright red tie and glasses as thick as Coke bottles. When he called out his greeting, the people in the crowded theater called back, cheering and shouting.

"You tell 'em, Nat D."

"Let's get going, now."

"Bring 'em out, man."

The orchestra started to play, and the audience joined in, singing the "Beale Street Blues," rocking back and forth in their seats. When they finished, Nat D. held up his hand.

"Folks, you know the rules. We bring on the acts, and you vote by cheering or booing or carrying on. At the end of the night, the winner gets five dollars, second place gets three, and third place gets two.

"All right, I guarantee you're going to love this show tonight. If you don't love it, maybe it'll make you laugh. If you don't laugh, just try not to shoot anybody. That's the job of the Lord High Executioner."

He gestured toward the wings, and a man stepped out wearing a top hat and carrying a pearl-handled revolver. He raised the gun and fired off a couple of shots, which I was hoping were blanks. The crowd went wild.

Nat D. told a few jokes, then introduced the first act. It was a young man who juggled water balloons. He got three in the air, then four, but when he tried for five something went wrong. One balloon broke, then another. The crowd laughed and booed. Somebody threw a tomato, and it splattered on the stage. The Lord High Executioner stepped out and fired off a shot. The young man was so startled that he dropped the other balloons. He stood there in a puddle of water, blinking at the audience. Finally he gathered up the pieces of rubber and walked off.

Nat D. introduced the other acts, one by one. There was a kazoo player, a jug band, and a one-legged dancer.

There was a man who wore a turban and charmed snakes. And there were blues singers of every size and shape. Some of the singers were greeted with tomatoes and some with gunshots. A few sounded good enough to be on the radio.

As the music played, I looked around and was surprised to see another white face. Standing against the wall a few feet away from me was a white boy several years older than I was. The first thing I noticed about him was his hair. It was long and slicked down, but it kept falling into his eyes. Every few minutes he would reach up and sweep it back over his forehead. The second thing I noticed was his clothes. Instead of jeans and a T-shirt, or khakis and a button-down collar, he was wearing a glittery pink shirt, black pants with a pink stripe down the leg, and black-and-white two-toned shoes. I'd seen a lot of clothes like that on Beale Street, but the people wearing them had been Negroes.

As the acts continued onstage, the white boy's eyes darted nervously around the room. He leaned forward, head bobbing, knee bouncing, his fingers drumming against the wall, like a hot rodder revving his engine.

During a break I saw him slip into the lobby. Curious, I found myself following. There was a poster of a guitar player named B. B. King, and he stopped in front of it. I went over and stood next to him, looking up at the poster.

"Have you ever heard him?" I asked.

The boy smiled shyly. "Sure have. Right here at the Palace."

"Is he good?"

"I reckon he's the best," said the boy. He cast his eyes down, as if the knowledge embarrassed him. "They say he used to do amateur nights. Had busted-up shoes and a raggedy guitar. He'd play just to get the prize money. Course, that was before 'Three O'Clock Blues.'"

"What's that?" I asked.

"A record. Number one on the R&B charts in 1951."

He took out a pack of gum and offered me a stick. I took one, and so did he.

"Do you come here much?" I asked.

"Beale Street? Sure."

I said, "It's a different kind of place."

He smiled. There was glass over the poster, and he glanced in it to see his reflection.

"I like it," he said. I couldn't tell if he meant Beale Street or the reflection.

"Where'd you get the shirt?" I asked.

"At Lansky's. Pants and shoes, too."

"Lansky's?" I said. The name sounded familiar.

He said, "Listen to Dewey Phillips. He'll tell you about it."

Then I remembered. *Lansky Brothers Clothing, down on Beale Street.*

"Oh, yeah," I said. "I listen to him."

"That man's crazy. He's the best. Well, you know."

I nodded. "Yeah, I know."

He pushed the hair out of his eyes, then put his hands in his pockets and started jiggling the change, his knee still bouncing.

"My name's Johnny Ross," I said.

He took his hand from his pocket and shook mine.

"I'm Elvis," he said. "Elvis Presley."

The name fit. It was as strange as his appearance.

"Rufus Thomas started here too," said Elvis. "So did Furry Lewis."

"Do they play the blues?"

"Oh, yeah," he said. "Oh, yeah."

He looked around, as if checking to see if anybody was listening. Then he said, "So do I."

I wasn't sure I'd heard him right. "Pardon me?"

He shrugged. "I'm a singer." On his face was a little sideways smile, almost a smirk. "If you'd been here last Tuesday night you would have heard me."

I stared at him. "You sang at amateur night?"

He ducked his head and nodded.

I tried to imagine a white boy on the stage of the Palace Theater, singing to a room full of Negroes. For some reason it made me laugh. I covered my mouth, but I couldn't seem to stop.

"I'm sorry," I said.

Elvis smiled. "That's all right. It's what they did, too."

I laughed again, and he joined in with a shy chuckle. Then he said, "Not all of them laughed. I think the girls liked it. At least they didn't throw tomatoes."

I said, "You really sing the blues?"

"I sing all kinds—blues, pop, country, gospel . . ."

"Gospel? You mean, Negro church music?"

He said, "You ever hear Reverend Brewster on WHBQ?"

I shook my head. I didn't know what he was talking about.

"Oh, man," said Elvis, "you got to hear him. Sunday

nights he does a radio broadcast from East Trigg Baptist Church, off Bellevue. There's a singer named Queen C. Anderson. She'll put you in the clouds."

"How do you know this stuff?" I asked.

"It's all around," he said. "I just listen."

Inside the theater, somebody was playing the piano. There was a gunshot.

"Are you going back in?" I asked.

"Nah. You want to go outside?"

"Okay," I said.

Out on Beale, the sidewalk was still crowded. We walked toward Main Street, past billiard parlors and pawnshops.

"Where do you go to school?" asked Elvis.

"Central. How about you?"

"I graduated last year from Humes. I work at Crown Electric, over on Poplar."

One storefront was crowded with people, and recorded music floated out the door. On the window was a sign that said HENRY'S RECORD SHOP AND SHINE PARLOR.

"That's the best record store on Beale Street," said Elvis. "All the musicians go there."

"You buy records?" I asked.

He laughed. "I surely do."

We walked on a little farther, and he said, "I made one, too."

"Huh?"

"I made a record." He said it casually, the way you might comment on the weather. I could tell it wasn't casual, though, because he glanced at me to see my reaction.

I stared at him. "When? Where?"

"There's a place over on Union, the Memphis Recording Service. They have a label called Sun Records. I cut a record called 'My Happiness.'"

"You mean, an actual record?" I said.

He flashed that one-sided smile. "You can hear it sometime if you want."

I said, "My mother sings that song. It's not Negro music."

"I told you, man, I sing all kinds."

"Did you make money on it?" I asked.

Elvis sized me up, like he was trying to decide how much to tell me. He said, "Truth is, I paid them. If you give them $3.98, they'll make a record for you. But the owner, Mr. Phillips, he liked my voice."

"Dewey Phillips?" I said. "You know him?"

He shook his head. "Sam Phillips. No relation. But they're good friends. Dewey goes by there all the time."

"Have you met him?" I asked.

"Not yet," said Elvis. "Anyway, Mr. Phillips called me back last Saturday. Said he had a song for me, called 'Without You.' We worked on it awhile, then he had me sing some other things. Everything I knew, seemed like. I was there three hours."

"And what happened?"

"Nothing, so far," he said.

We came to a lime green Lincoln coupe parked at the corner. Elvis pulled some keys from his pocket.

"I gotta go," he said.

I shrugged. "It was good to meet you."

"Maybe I'll see you again," he said.

He got into the coupe, checked his hair in the mirror, then started the engine and pulled away from the curb, his elbow hooked over the door. Turning right on Main, he gave me a little nod and headed off into the night.

CHAPTER THREE

I wandered around Beale Street a while longer, spent some time in Schwab's, then walked up to Union Avenue and caught a bus home.

I was gazing out the bus window, looking at the darkened stores but not really seeing them, when something caught my eye. A small building was lit up brightly, in spite of the fact that it was ten thirty at night. Curious, I tried to look in the window, but the blinds were drawn. Over the window was a small neon sign that said MEMPHIS RECORDING SERVICE.

Without thinking, I reached up and pulled the cord. A bell rang, and the bus stopped at the next corner. I got off and hurried back to the building.

It was a one-story brick structure no more than thirty feet wide, with a glass door and two large windows, all of which were covered by venetian blinds. A light streamed out from behind the blinds. Somewhere far away I heard a man singing and a drum pounding.

I tried the door, but it was locked. Backing up, I looked at the place to see if there might be another entrance. Next door, on the corner, was a restaurant on the first floor of a two-story building. The restaurant was closed, but a driveway led toward the back. I followed it to a gravel parking lot behind the two buildings. A few beat-up cars were parked there, illuminated by a light from the restaurant.

The singing was louder now, and I could make out a guitar and piano, playing along with the drums. The back door of the little building was open. I moved closer. The music rose up to meet me, rough and hard. The man's voice was ragged, but somehow it was also strong: *"Well, raisin' a good cotton crop just like a lucky man shootin' dice."*

Inside the door was a machine with two reels of tape turning steadily. Beside it, a wavy-haired man hunched over a console that was covered by rows of dials and switches. Needles moved in two illuminated meters, bouncing upward with every note. The man's hands danced across the console, adjusting dials, caressing the metal.

Beyond the console was a window made of thick glass. Through the window, in an adjoining room, I saw four men, all of them Negroes, spread out around a microphone. The singer, a man whose face was lined and scarred, wore an old work shirt that was rolled up above his elbows, with rings of sweat under the arms. Behind him, an elderly piano player sat up straight and tall, eyes closed, pounding out chords, as the drummer, a broad barn of a man, beat on a snare like he was chopping wood. Next to the singer was a guitar player, an angry-looking man with coal black skin, bad teeth, and hair that stuck out from his head when he played.

The singer finished his verse and turned to the guitar player, who stepped forward with a scowl on his face. He jerked out a kink in the electrical cord that went from his guitar to a dented amplifier and, eyes flashing, began to flay away at the guitar. The sound that came out took my breath away. It was like a scream, like a bellow full of pain and rage. His anger came pouring through his fingers, into the guitar, and out the amp, distorted like the expression on his face. The sound shook and wailed and pounded like a clenched fist. I wanted to cover my ears, but I was afraid I might miss something.

When the song ended, the man at the console stopped the tape machine. He leaned over to a small microphone next to the console and pushed a button.

"Whoo-ee! Whatever y'all are drinking in there, can I have me a sip?"

The singer laughed. He pulled a handkerchief from his back pocket and wiped his forehead. The guitar player, still scowling, sat down on the amp. He reached for a paper cup and took a drink from it. The man at the console got to his feet, opened a door next to him, and went into the adjoining room. The microphone in there was still on, so I was able to hear what they said.

"I believe we got a good one," the man told the group.

"I could see that cotton," said the piano player. "Lord, it was so real it made my fingers hurt."

The man said, "Okay, fellas, let's take a break. James, you got anything else?"

"I don't know," said the singer. "Let me think about it."

The guitar player said, "I got one."

"What is it?" asked the man.

"'I'm Gonna Murder My Baby.'"

The drummer said, "Yeah, but what's the name of your song?" Grinning, he looked at the others. They glanced away nervously.

"That is the name of my song," the guitar player told him. "Something wrong with that?"

"Not a thing," said the drummer. "Not a thing."

The wavy-haired man started fiddling with the microphone, and the musicians filed through the door, headed for the parking lot. For a second I considered ducking behind a car, but then I changed my mind. I wanted to stand next to the people who had made that music. I wanted to see them up close.

The drummer was the first one out. Spotting me, he said, "Well, looka here."

The others didn't seem too interested. Pulling out cigarettes, they lit up.

"I like your music," I said.

"Oh, yeah?" said the guitar player. "Well, it ain't free."

The drummer turned to me, a gleam in his eye. "Maybe we could work out a deal. You know, an admission fee."

"Like what?" I said.

"There's a bottle of Jack Daniels by the microphone," said the drummer. "Bring it here."

When people tell me to do something, usually it makes

me want to do the opposite. Somehow this seemed differ-ent. It was like he was daring me to do it, like he was test-ing my nerve. Besides, I wanted to see what was inside.

"Okay," I said.

I went through the door, past the console, and into the adjoining room. It was an odd-shaped space with a linoleum floor and acoustic tiles on the walls and ceiling. The piano and drums were set up by the window that looked into the first room, and the guitar was propped up against the amplifier. Nearby was the microphone, and next to that was a bottle of Jack Daniels.

Off to my left was a door into a front room. The door was pushed halfway shut, and beyond it I could hear some-one rummaging around, humming a tune. Moving quickly, I stepped toward the microphone to get the bottle. As I reached for it, the door opened.

"Hey, what are you doing?"

I looked up. The wavy-haired man stood in the door-way. My hand glanced off the side of the bottle, knocking it over, and whiskey poured out.

"Oh, man," I said. "Sorry."

I grabbed for the bottle and set it back up, but a puddle had formed and was spreading across the floor. Looking around desperately, I saw a newspaper that had been flung into the corner. I got it and used the pages to blot up the whiskey.

The man stood in the doorway, watching me. "We got enough trouble around here without kids stealing our booze. Why don't you break a few windows while you're at it? Grab some hubcaps."

I said, "I wasn't stealing anything. The drummer asked me to bring him the bottle."

"I'm supposed to believe that?"

"Believe what you want. It's true."

The man looked me over. "Then do it," he said.

I moved toward the back door, stooping to pick up the whiskey bottle on my way out. I carried it to the parking lot and gave it to the drummer. He smiled.

"Hey, I like that," he said. He tipped back the bottle and took a swig.

I went back inside and looked around. The wavy-haired man was at the microphone, which he had taken off the stand and was adjusting with a small tool.

"Who are you?" he asked. "What are you doing here?"

"I'm Johnny Ross. I've been listening to the music."

"Oh, yeah? What do you think?"

"I like it."

He cocked his head and studied me. "Why?"

"I don't know. It seems real."

He nodded his head toward the instruments. "You know what this is, don't you?"

"A recording session?"

"It's history," he said. "The men out there, they didn't write those songs. They lived them. They worked in the hot sun picking cotton, like their people been doing for a hundred years. And they could be the last ones. Go to the Delta now, what do you see? Machines. Machines do the picking. The people can't find jobs, so they come to Memphis. They clean houses, do yard work. If they're like James Cotton, they sing. It's all in his voice. It's all there. We try to get it on tape."

I said, "James Cotton? Is that really his name?"

The man smiled. "That's right. Everything about him is cotton. He picks cotton in his sleep. He dreams about it, I guarantee you."

"Who's the guitar player?" I asked.

He glanced toward the door and lowered his voice. "That, my friend, is the loudest, meanest, rawest musician in Memphis. His name is Pat Hare. You watch out for him, hear?"

James Cotton. Pat Hare. They sounded like characters out of a children's story, but they sure didn't act like it.

"Well?" said the man.

I looked back at him, puzzled. "Well what?"

"Where's your manners, boy? You wanted to know their names. Aren't you going to ask mine?"

I said, "You're Sam Phillips. This is Sun Records."

He straightened his shoulders, and his face brightened. "How'd you know?"

"A friend of mine told me. Elvis Presley."

"Oh, yeah," he said. "Presley. Strange kid."

He shook his head, then went back to work. Pretty soon he looked up again. "Will you stop staring? Do something. Make yourself useful."

Looking around, I picked up the newspapers and put them in the trash. As I worked, I had an idea. Ordinarily it wasn't the kind of thing I'd say out loud, but nothing about this night had been ordinary.

"Mr. Phillips," I said, "I've been looking for work. You wouldn't have anything around here, would you?"

He laughed. "You want a job?"

"I'm sixteen years old," I lied. "I can do plenty of things."

"Yeah," he said, "you're doing great so far."

"You wouldn't have to pay me much."

He thought about it for a minute. "Well, it's like this," he said. "Just two of us work here, and some weeks we go without pay. Things are looking up, though. Word's getting around. People like James Cotton hear about us. They come by, and maybe we cut a record. Maybe it sells. I can't offer you a job tonight, but if you're willing to come back and help out around the studio on a volunteer basis, I'll give it some thought. No promises, though. You understand?"

"Yes, sir. Yes, sir, I do. I really appreciate it."

He clapped me on the back. "Now, go out back and get those fellas in here. We got some history to make."

CHAPTER FOUR

I slept late the next morning. When I got up, there was a note from my mother beside the bed, saying I had looked tired and so she had let me sleep. She probably knew I'd been out late, but this morning, for a change, I didn't feel guilty about it.

Thinking back to the night before, I pictured the look on Sam Phillips's face as he sat at the console. I recalled the way his hands had danced across the dials. Most of all, I remembered the music. After James Cotton had finished, Pat Hare had recorded his song, which really was called "I'm Gonna Murder My Baby."

In the song Hare's girlfriend had cheated on him, and he was going after her. But if he loved her, would he really kill her? How could loving and killing go together?

Climbing out of bed, I headed for the kitchen, where I got some toast and jam. I finished them, then pulled on some clothes and took the bus along Union Avenue to Sun

Records. I was expecting to go around back, like the night before, but today the blinds were open in front and the lights were on.

I walked by the restaurant, which was doing a good business, and went next door to Sun. I hadn't entered from the street or seen the front room, so I didn't know what to expect. I had visions of hungover musicians staggering around the place, smoking and carrying liquor bottles. Instead, I found a neat reception area and a desk with flowers in a vase. Behind the desk was a blond-haired woman with a pretty smile.

I looked around to make sure I was in the right place. "Is this Sun Records?"

"Yes, it is. Can I help you?"

I said, "My name is Johnny Ross. I talked to Mr. Phillips last night. He said he might consider me for a job."

"Oh, yes, he mentioned you."

"He did?"

The woman came out from behind the desk and extended her hand. "I'm Marion Keisker. I work with Mr. Phillips." She shook hands the way a man would— strong, with no hesitation.

I studied her face. "I think I've seen you before."

"Did you ever listen to *Meet Kitty Kelly*?" she asked.

"On the radio? It used to be one of my mother's favorite programs."

She smiled. "I was Kitty."

I looked more closely at her. "Now I remember," I said. "It was at the Peabody Hotel. You used to eat lunch there."

"You've got a good memory. The studios were in the basement of the hotel. That's where I met Sam Phillips. Radio station WREC. He was the engineer on some of my programs."

"How did you get here?" I asked.

"Sam decided to open a recording studio and asked me to join him. I was crazy enough to say yes." She shrugged. "I was ready for a change. Starting a new business sounded like fun. And Sam—well, he's a genius."

"Is he here?"

"Not yet. He'll probably be in this afternoon."

I glanced around the office. "I really would like a job. Is there something I can help you with?"

"Well, as long as you're asking, the studio's a mess. That must have been quite a session last night."

She showed me where the supplies were, and I got started on the studio. I worked for most of the morning, cleaning and straightening up. I tried to get rid of the Jack Daniels smell and finally decided it must be a permanent feature of the place, pounded into the walls along with the drumbeats.

Around lunchtime I heard voices coming from the front room. One was Marion's. The other one, a man's voice, was familiar but I couldn't place it. I opened the door and looked in.

It was Elvis Presley. The night before, I'd been so struck by his appearance that I hadn't noticed his voice. It was low and smooth, like Bing Crosby with a twang. As for his flashy clothes, they had been replaced by a Crown Electric uniform, made up of work pants and a short-sleeved shirt with his name stitched over the pocket. Somehow, though, he still managed to look different. Maybe it was the alligator belt and two-toned shoes.

Elvis stared at me. "What are you doing here?"

"You two know each other?" asked Marion.

I told her how we had met and what he had said about Sun Records.

"He's the reason I'm here," I said.

"What about you, Elvis?" she said with a twinkle in her eye. "Why are you here?"

Elvis blushed. "Aw, now, Miss Marion, you know why. I want to make records."

Marion said, "Elvis drops by nearly every day, trying to butter me up and get back in the studio."

"What do you think?" he said. "Is it working?"

"You're getting close," she said. "Just a few more flowers and a box of candy."

Elvis said, "Man, thinking about candy makes me hungry. You want some lunch, Johnny? I could drive us someplace. I've got a truck from work."

I looked at Marion, and she nodded.

"If you're interested, come back Friday afternoon," she told me. "There's another recording session."

"I'll be here." Turning to Elvis, I said, "How about K's?"

K's Kreem was a drive-in place on Crump Boulevard. Any day of the summer you'd find the parking lot full of teenagers, eating, talking, listening to music. K's had the best shakes in town, but my reason for going there had nothing to do with food.

Elvis guided his Crown Electric truck into the parking lot, and a few minutes later a waitress appeared. As she turned toward us, I saw her face. It was Ruth Ann Morris.

After seeing her at Poplar Tunes, I had done some checking around. I had learned that her father was a mechanic and her mother taught Sunday school. Ruth Ann had gotten a summer job at K's to help out with family finances.

She was wearing one of those pink waitress outfits with a little pointed hat. On anyone else it might have looked silly, but not on her. She approached the truck, sparkling like a star.

"Johnny!" she said. "Wow, twice in a week."

"Yeah, what a coincidence," I said.

Next to me, Elvis wore a shy, sideways grin.

"This is my friend, Elvis Presley," I told her. "He's not really a truck driver. He's a singer. Right, Elvis?"

"I sing a little bit," he said.

She took my order. Then Elvis asked for two cheeseburgers, fries, onion rings, and a chocolate milk shake. When it came time to pay, he discovered he was short of money, so I lent him some.

We got our food and took it to one of the picnic tables at the side of the parking lot. As we ate, I told him what had happened at Sun Records the night before.

"I met Sam Phillips," I said. "He was working with James Cotton and Pat Hare."

Elvis said, "Man, they're two of the best bluesmen in Memphis." He asked for details, and I described how I had met them and helped Sam in the studio. As I spoke, I had trouble keeping the excitement out of my voice.

He looked at me and grinned. "You caught it, didn't you? The blues."

I said, "It's not like other music. I listened to Eddie Arnold this morning. It wasn't the same."

"No, man, you're ruined for Eddie Arnold. It's too late. You got the bug."

Sipping my drink, I gazed out across the parking lot. "Sometimes I get this feeling when I listen to it. Like I'm looking for something. Like maybe it's close by, but I can't see it."

"Oh, yeah," said Elvis.

"I don't even know what it is. I just want it. You ever get that feeling?"

Elvis followed my gaze. For a minute he stared where I was staring, as if the thing was out there taking shape. His eyes were veiled, but in them I glimpsed something hard and bright, like the gleam of a diamond.

"I'm going to find it," he said.

As he spoke, a Cadillac convertible pulled into the lot. Inside were Trey Chapman and Graydon Scarborough. I'd never actually met Graydon, but I'd seen him around. He was Trey's designated cheerleader and comedian. They pulled into a spot next to our table.

"Who's your friend, Johnny?" asked Trey from the car.

"This is Elvis Presley," I said.

Graydon said, "Elvis? What kind of name is that?"

"It's my daddy's middle name," said Elvis.

I said, "This is Trey Chapman and Graydon Scarborough. They live in my neighborhood."

Trey said, "Actually, he lives in ours." He turned to Graydon. "Johnny's mother works for my old man. She's a secretary."

"Bookkeeper," I said. "She's the bookkeeper."

Trey shrugged. "We let him and his mother stay in back."

"Why?" asked Graydon.

"I'm not sure," said Trey. "I've never been able to figure that out."

Graydon looked me over. "Where's your father?"

I didn't answer, because I didn't know. He was gone. I'd never met him, but I didn't want to say it.

Trey said, "He used to be our chauffeur. When she got pregnant, he ran off."

"He had his reasons," I said.

Graydon noticed Elvis's food. "Hey, onion rings." Getting out of the car, he stepped over the table and tried one. "These are good. You want one, Trey?"

"They're not yours," I said.

Ignoring me, Graydon said, "Hey, Elvis, I like your outfit. Where do you work?"

"Crown Electric."

"I know them," said Graydon. "They fixed the heater in our swimming pool."

Elvis didn't say anything. He just sipped on his milk shake.

Graydon said, "Trey, look at this. He's got a shirt with his name on it. Fancy, huh? And check this out. Two-toned shoes. Where'd you get those, Elvis?"

"Lansky's," said Elvis. "Down on Beale."

Graydon said, "Beale Street? You go down there?"

"That's right."

"Trey, you hear that? He likes Negroes. He shops with them."

Trey asked Elvis, "You ever go to any of those clubs? You know, where they sing the blues?"

"Yeah, I do," said Elvis.

I said, "So do I."

Trey raised his eyebrows. "Little Johnny Ross on Beale Street?" He was smirking, but I could tell he was surprised.

"Johnny works at Sun Records," said Elvis. "They record the blues."

Trey gazed at me. Graydon laughed. "Man, that's jungle music." He hopped around the area like a monkey, hooting and scratching under his arms.

"Cut it out," I said.

"Look, man," said Elvis, "we were just having some lunch. We don't want to bother nobody."

Graydon said, "Bother? Oh, it's no bother." He took another onion ring and popped it into his mouth. When he reached for one more, I stood up and grabbed his wrist.

"Stop," I said.

Graydon yanked his wrist free. I fell back against the table, spilling my drink. Without thinking, I buried my right fist in his stomach.

The breath exploded from his lungs. His eyes shot open and he crumpled to the ground, gasping for air. I stared at him, surprised at what I'd done.

Trey climbed slowly out of the car. Standing over Graydon, he eyed me with interest. There was something about the way he did it, something I couldn't identify. Then he glanced at Graydon.

"Get up," he said.

Reaching down, Trey grabbed him under one arm and yanked him, still gasping, to his feet. I heard a noise behind us and looked back to see a man approaching. He was wearing an apron and hat.

"What's going on here?" he asked. Then he noticed Trey. "Hey, Trey, how you doing?"

Trey nodded. "I'm fine, K. Everything's fine here."

It was the owner, Ruth Ann's boss. He glanced at Graydon and back at Trey.

"Okay," he said. "Just checking. Say hello to your dad, huh?"

When the man left, Trey turned to Graydon, Elvis, and me.

"Here's the deal," said Trey. "You don't tell your friends. You don't tell your parents. As far as you're concerned, nothing happened. Got it?"

I nodded. Elvis nodded. Graydon wheezed.

As they got back in the car, Ruth Ann approached. I grinned, and she shot me a little smile. Trey saw it. He gazed at me for a minute, then turned to Ruth Ann.

"Hey, baby," he said.

My face flushed. I took a step toward Trey.

So did Ruth Ann. She checked to make sure her boss wasn't watching, then leaned in and gave Trey a kiss on the lips. He pinched her, and she giggled.

Straightening her hat, she pulled out her order pad. "Can I get you something?"

"Nah," said Trey. "We were just leaving. I'll pick you up after work."

He pulled her close for another kiss, then looked right at me, a cocky grin on his face. Putting the car in gear, he pulled out of the lot. Ruth Ann watched him all the way.

As he drove off, I remembered what Elvis had told me. I had caught it, all right. I had the blues.

That afternoon, I couldn't stop thinking about Ruth Ann. I remembered how Trey had pulled her close and kissed her. All the while I heard the blues. It played in my head, soothing me, mocking me, telling how it was.

I went back to Beale Street that night. As I moved along the sidewalk, I heard a harmonica. Instead of being slow and sad, it played music that jumped and throbbed. Sometimes it chugged like a train. Sometimes it roared and screamed. It punched the air, then backed off and rocked side to side, bending notes, stretching them, spitting them out like tobacco juice.

I looked up and saw a banged-up door. Above it was a sign that said THE GREY MULE. I tried to go in, but the man at the door stopped me.

"Boy, what you doing?" he said. "Go on home now."

The harmonica kept playing, cutting through the night. As I listened, I got an idea. I made my way to the corner, where I turned and walked up half a block. There was an alley, just as I had hoped. I plunged in, moving along quickly, listening for the harmonica. Sure enough, there it was, coming through the back door of the club.

I peered inside. It was a small room filled with yellow

light and cigarette smoke. A half-dozen tables were scattered through the place, and people were gathered around them, talking and drinking. There were three musicians in an open space by the bar—a pianist, a bass player, and the man on harmonica. The man wore a panama hat pulled down low over his face. His hands were wrapped around a small harmonica, pushing and pulling, tugging at the notes, jamming them together and then stringing them out like beads.

As much as the hands fascinated me, it was the man's legs I kept staring at. Lean and limber, wrapped in loose-fitting purple slacks, they swung and stretched and whipped and gyrated, knees bumping together and circling out again, always moving, never standing still, the pant legs flapping like flags.

A woman at one of the tables must have been watching them too. She yelled, "Get it, baby. Shake 'em. Shake 'em, now."

As I watched and listened, I found myself moving with the beat. Then the light shifted and the man looked up, his face suddenly illuminated. I stopped moving. For a moment, so did the man.

I was staring at Lamont Turner, and he was staring back.

CHAPTER FIVE

Lamont stood beside me, hands on his hips.

"What are you doing?" he demanded.

It was the same thing I had asked Lamont the day before when I'd found him in my front yard, and the meaning was the same: This place is mine.

"Just listening," I said. "It's a free world."

"The world's not free," he said. "Never was, never will be."

We stood in the alley outside the back door of the Grey Mule. When Lamont had seen me a few minutes earlier, he had murmured something to the piano player, then hurried out the door to confront me. As I studied him now, the piano powered through the chorus, with the bass matching him note for note.

I said, "I didn't know you played music."

"There's a lot you don't know about me," he said.

"Does Will know?"

"My father? He knows everything. Didn't he tell you?"
I saw a flash of silver in his hand.

"Can I look at your harmonica?" I asked.

He grunted. "Man, don't call it a harmonica. That's what little kids play. It's a harp."

"How do you do it?" I asked. "How do you make it sound like that?"

I imagined myself in the Grey Mule, facing the crowd, playing the instrument called a harp, moving my legs the way Lamont did.

"It takes practice," he said. "It's hard work."

"You think I could do it?"

"You could play the harp if you practiced," he said. "You couldn't play the blues."

The music ended, and the crowd shouted its approval. The piano player got up from his chair and came to the door.

"Lamont? Come on, man, we need you."

Lamont turned to me. "I got to go."

"You mind if I stay and listen?"

He shrugged. "Suit yourself."

He adjusted his hat, then went back in. I waited until he started playing again, then stepped through the door while no one was watching. Sometime around midnight, Lamont and his friends finished and another group came on. Lamont saw me on his way out the back door.

"You still here?"

"That was great," I said.

"You're lucky they didn't throw you out."

"Where did you learn to play like that?"

He looked me over, then reached into his pocket and pulled out some keys. "My Ford's parked in back. If you want to go for a ride, the offer still stands."

I hesitated, and he sighed. "Come on, man. I promise not to beat you up."

The Ford was dark blue, the color of night. Brightly polished, it sparkled under the streetlights. I got in and found the interior clean and neatly kept.

Lamont climbed in behind the wheel. Taking off his panama hat, he placed it carefully on the backseat. When he started the engine, there was a low, rumbling sound like the growl of a leopard. He pulled away from the curb and drove up to Fourth Street, where he turned south.

It seemed strange being alone in the car with a Negro. I saw Negroes all the time. I talked with them. Sometimes we bumped elbows. But this felt different, more personal, maybe because it was his car.

"How did you get the car?" I asked.

"Stole it," said Lamont.

I studied him. "No, really," I said.

He smiled. With Lamont, I was starting to learn that everything was a test—whether I would shake his hand, go driving with him, or believe he was a thief. So far it seemed that I had passed.

Lamont said, "It's my mother's car. We have a deal. I can use it as long as I keep it running."

"You're a mechanic, like Will?" I asked.

Lamont shook his head. "It's different. He fixes other people's cars. I fix ours."

I said, "Well, are you going to tell me?"

"Tell you what?"

"Where did you learn to play like that?"

He said, "Chicago, south side. I used to go to the clubs down there. There was a harp player named Dusty Brown. One night I went up to him between sets. Asked if he could teach me to play. He must have seen something in me, because he invited me to his house. Old Dusty, he taught me everything I know. Except the blues. Nobody can teach you that."

We passed Linden Avenue. "Where are we going?" I asked.

"Just riding. Making some breeze."

He had rolled down the windows, and hot air whipped through the car. Of course, it was an illusion. The air just sat there. We were the ones blowing through the night.

Farther on, a group of low buildings rose up on our left.

"Ever seen those before?" asked Lamont.

"I don't think so."

"It's Foote Homes, a housing project. The city built it fifteen years ago. Four square blocks of concrete boxes. 'Nice homes for Negroes.' That's what the city said. Less than a mile from here is another housing project, Lauderdale Courts. It's for white people. Which one do you think is nicer?"

A light flickered in front of one apartment. It grew bigger and brighter as I watched.

"What's that light?" I said.

Lamont approached the apartment and slowed down. On the lawn, a cross was burning.

I glanced at Lamont. He stared, orange light flickering

across his face. Then he yanked on the wheel and pulled up to the curb. Slamming on the brakes, he jumped out of the car, and I jumped with him.

By that time the cross, about five feet high, was completely engulfed in flames. At its center were the letters *KKK*. I knew what those letters stood for. So did everyone in Memphis. It was the Ku Klux Klan.

I glanced around to see who else was there and noticed two white boys in the shadows, running to a green Chevrolet that was parked across the street. As I watched, they got in and pulled away. I tried to make out their faces, but it was too dark.

"Fire!" yelled Lamont. "There's a fire!"

Lights turned on. Heads poked out of windows. The flames rose higher, coming dangerously close to the building.

I had heard stories of the Ku Klux Klan burning crosses to intimidate Negroes, but most of the stories were from years ago. Occasionally you'd hear about a Klan meeting out in the country someplace, where people in robes would complain about Negroes, make angry threats, and burn a cross at someone's house as a warning. But this cross was right here, right now, singeing the grass, throwing heat on my face.

"Get a hose!" somebody yelled.

A woman came running up, dragging a hose, but there was no faucet. Lamont found one around the side of the building, but when he hooked up the hose there was no pressure. Finally I heard sirens in the distance, and a fire truck pulled around the corner.

Firemen leaped off the truck. Behind them, I saw a green shape drift by and stop. It was the Chevrolet.

"Lamont!" I yelled.

He looked up from the dry faucet.

I pointed at the Chevrolet. "They did it."

Suddenly he was sprinting across the lawn, digging the keys from his pocket, and I was right next to him. We threw open the car doors, hopped inside, and tore out into the street. The Chevrolet was just disappearing around the corner at Mississippi Street. Lamont accelerated, leaning over the wheel, and we skidded down Mississippi after them.

"Go faster," I said.

"Shut up," said Lamont. He was operating in a tightly contained world, made up of his eyes, his hands, the steering wheel, and a long narrow tunnel to the green Chevrolet.

"What'll we do if we catch them?" I asked.

He didn't answer. Judging by the look in his eyes, it was nothing those white boys would care to discover.

We followed them down Mississippi to Butler, then west to Avery and Vance. Lamont was a good driver, but the white boy was better, and the distance between us grew. Lamont shook his head in frustration.

"You saw them," he said. "What did they look like?"

I tried to call up an image, but it was no use. My memories were a blur. Watching the car, I had a thought.

"The license plate!" I said. "Let's get the tag number."

Lamont nodded. "You get the first three numbers. I'll get the last three."

He edged up closer to the Chevrolet. I studied the plate. 2-2-0. I said it over and over again to myself.

We hurtled north on Third, then east again on Linden. The Chevrolet pulled steadily away. At Hernando Street we gave up the chase, the rear lights disappearing into the distance.

I said, "2-2-0."

Lamont said, "4-2-3."

He smiled grimly.

CHAPTER SIX

It was lunchtime at the Peabody Hotel. Waiters in tuxedos glided around the room, carrying food and speaking in low voices. Seated at the tables were some of the richest people in Memphis. Then there was us.

My mother and I were in our usual place, off in a corner by the kitchen where the head waiter had seated us. He saw us every week but had never once smiled or said hello. Even so, my mother greeted him like an old friend.

"Why do you do that?" I asked her when the waiter left.

"Do what?"

"Talk to him that way. He doesn't care about us."

"He's a nice man," she said.

"He knows we don't belong."

Thursday was payday, the one day of the week when my mother could afford to eat lunch at the Peabody Hotel. It was the fanciest hotel in town, the place where you went if you wanted to see and be seen. My mother liked to go there, soak up the atmosphere, and pretend to be rich. Only problem was, she didn't like eating alone. That was where I came in. I met her there every week. I didn't care much about the Peabody, but I enjoyed being downtown.

I watched the waiter hurry off to help another customer, a lady wearing enough jewelry for ten people. The waiter smiled and bowed as he helped her off with her fur.

I said, "Why would anyone wear a fur during the summer?"

My mother didn't hear me. She was busy looking at the menu. I don't know why, since she always ordered the same thing, a Waldorf salad. Personally, I didn't think she even cared how it tasted. She just liked the name.

I always ordered the same thing too. It was a grilled cheese sandwich, the one item on the menu guaranteed to make the waiter frown.

"Somebody burned a cross at Foote Homes last night," I said.

"Where did you hear that?"

"Lamont told me. You know, Will's son."

She looked up from the menu, her eyes flashing. "I told you to stay away from him."

"He said it was a big cross on one of the lawns. It had *KKK* carved on it."

"I don't care what he said. He's off limits. You hear me?"

"Why?" I said.

She sat there, staring at me. I knew that look. The last time her face had that expression, I'd been grounded for a week. With the summer just starting, I couldn't afford that now.

"All right," I said. "Fine."

She nodded. Setting down her menu, she leaned back in her chair and looked around the room.

"You know," she said, "they used to have dances here on Saturday night. There was a live band, with flowers and champagne. It was lovely."

"How do you know?" I asked.

"I used to go."

I tried to picture my mother at the Peabody, surrounded by flowers, whirling around the dance floor.

"Don't look so surprised," she said, smiling. "I wasn't always a mother. I used to go out a lot. You know, kick up my heels. Have some fun."

As hard as I tried, I couldn't imagine it. The woman I knew worked late and went to bed early. She cooked meals and set rules.

"Who did you go with?" I asked. "Was it my father?"

She hesitated. "Yes," she said.

In my mind, his face was out of focus, like the photos I'd seen of him. We only had a few of the photos, and my mother kept them put away most of the time.

"You never talk about him. What was he like?"

"He was a fine man," she said.

"Then why did he leave?"

"I wish I knew."

The waiter came by and took our order. Gathering up the menus, he left without saying a word.

"What about you, Johnny?" she asked.

"What do you mean?"

"Are you having any fun?"

I thought of Ruth Ann and Trey. "Sure," I said.

She reached across the table and put her hand on mine. "Maybe once in a while you should kick up your heels, like I used to do."

I shrugged. "I'm fine."

"I hope so," she said.

"Next!" yelled Mr. Jack.

A big man with brown hair and a red face, he stood on the third floor of the National Cotton Company with his sleeves rolled up and his tie loosened, holding a clipboard and sweating. It was over ninety degrees outside, which meant it was over a hundred in the room.

National Cotton, like most of the companies on Cotton Row in downtown Memphis, was in a three-story brick building. On the first floor were the offices, where I had dropped off my mother after lunch. The second floor was for storage. The third floor, the classing floor, was where the business took place.

"Set 'em up," called Mr. Jack.

A group of Negro men with bulging muscles lugged in the next load of cotton, which was tied up in bales weighing up to five hundred pounds. The seller, an older man with a panama hat, said something to Mr. Jack, grinned nervously, and set a sample of his cotton on the classing table.

I watched Mr. Jack examine it. When I was a little boy he had taken a shine to me and let me follow him around the classing floor. These days, whenever I came into the office with my mother, I always went up to say hello. I liked it when he smiled at me, but it was more than that. Mr. Jack always said there was important business taking place in that room. Nearly half of all the cotton in the world was bought and sold by Memphis companies, and National Cotton was one of the biggest.

Mr. Jack made some notes on his clipboard and shook the seller's hand. As the next load was brought in, he noticed me and motioned me over.

"Hey there, Johnny," he said. "I got something for you."

He pulled something out of his pocket. It was a crisp dollar bill. Handing me the money, he said, "I believe this has your name on it."

I smiled. "Thank you, sir."

"Son, you take that to the Dairy Dip," he said. "They're saving a chocolate milk shake for you."

I grinned. "Yes, sir. Much obliged."

Heading for the stairs, I paused on the way to look out one of the windows that lined the back wall. A block away, stretching into the distance, was the Mississippi River. It was a mile wide at Memphis, brown and sluggish, and I could see Arkansas on the other side. Running along this side of the Mississippi was Riverside Drive, and beyond that was a slope down to the water, where barges were lined up, loading and unloading bales of cotton.

I went downstairs and out the front door. As I started up the sidewalk, a long, black Continental turned the corner and pulled up in front of the building. Will Turner got out of the driver's side, wearing a blue suit, a tie, and a cap. He was a tall, thin man of about forty, give or take a few years, with dark eyes, rough hands, graying hair, and light brown skin.

He came around to the curb side and opened the door. Out stepped Arthur Chapman. An elegant-looking man with silver hair and pale blue eyes, Mr. Chapman always wore a suit that was perfectly tailored, with a handkerchief in the front pocket. I heard that he ordered the suits from England, and each one cost more than a year's rent on our house.

Mr. Chapman said something to Will, then turned toward the building and saw me. He nodded briskly and brushed by me. "Hello, Johnny."

I thought of Trey and wondered if he and his father ever talked. I didn't think I'd ever seen Mr. Chapman have a real conversation with anyone. He mostly gave orders. I wondered what it would be like to have a father like that. I wondered what it would be like to have a father.

I looked at Will. "Hi," I said.

Will didn't answer. He got back in the car without saying a word and drove off down the street. He was quiet like that when Mr. Chapman was around. When I was younger it had hurt my feelings, but I had gotten used to it.

Mr. Chapman went inside, where he was met by one of his secretaries and escorted to his office. I turned away and headed up the sidewalk.

When I came downtown I usually wandered the streets

at a leisurely pace, watching the people and talking to the shopkeepers I knew. Today was different.

I hurried along Front Street to Madison and the downtown police station. At the desk I asked for Officer Barnes, the policeman Lamont and I had spoken to the night before. When we had returned to Foote Homes after the chase, two police officers had been there, taking names and information. I had been surprised to see that they were Negroes. Officer Barnes seemed to be the one in charge, and he'd been very interested in the license number we gave him. I had asked what would happen, and he had said to check at the downtown police station in the next day or two.

I told the man at the desk why I wanted to see Officer Barnes. The man disappeared into a back room, and when he came out a moment later, a white officer was with him.

"I'm Sergeant Linebaugh," he told me. "I'm handling that case."

"What about Officer Barnes?"

"He's back at the projects, patrolling."

"Did you find out whose license plate it was?" I asked.

Sergeant Linebaugh said, "Oh, so you're that kid. Barnes told me about you. What were you doing at Foote Homes?"

I shrugged. "Driving around."

"Kind of late, wasn't it?"

"I want to know who did it," I said. "Did you catch them yet?"

He eyed me coolly. "We're working on it," he said.

"Oh, and something else. That part of town? It's not for you. Stay away from there, you hear?"

As I left the police station, I thought about Sergeant Linebaugh's words. Lamont and I had helped by getting the tag number. He could have at least thanked us.

I wandered over to Confederate Park, a block-long oasis of green. Finding a bench, I watched the people around me. There was a young couple nearby, sitting on a blanket and playing with a baby boy. I could tell by the way they talked and smiled that they loved him and loved each other.

The man said something to the woman and then, grinning, picked up his son and swung him around in the air. The boy laughed, waving his arms in delight.

I wondered if my father had ever come to the park. Maybe he drove here sometimes after dropping off Mr. Chapman in the mornings. He might have parked the car, gotten out, and walked these same paths. He might have met my mother here for lunch, she in her pretty dress, he in his blue suit and cap. Maybe they sat on a bench and shared a sandwich, throwing the scraps to the pigeons.

I pictured the two of them at the Peabody Hotel and thought of what my mother had said. Kick up your heels. Have some fun. It gave me an idea.

Down the street from the park was a sandstone castle complete with turrets and a tower. If you squinted your eyes just right, you could see Queen Guinevere in the tower, waving to King Arthur and his knights. Of course, it wasn't really a castle. It was the city library.

Inside, I went to the reference desk and asked for a phone book. I looked up a number, then went to a pay phone. Taking out a pocketful of coins, I stacked them up next to the phone and dropped one into the slot. Then I took a deep breath and dialed the number of K's Kreem.

CHAPTER SEVEN

"Hey, Johnny, where you going?" called Trey.

It was Friday afternoon, and I was on my way to Sun Records for the recording session Marion had told me about. I was walking to the bus stop when Trey pulled up alongside me in his Cadillac. Graydon was with him.

"Going to work," I said.

"I'll take you there," said Trey. "Get in."

It was a hot day and I was sweating, but I didn't especially want to spend time with Trey and Graydon.

I shrugged. "Thanks, anyway. I'm fine."

"Get in," said Trey.

Graydon held open the door for me.

"Go to the back of the bus," he said, grinning.

Reluctantly, I climbed in back. On the seat next to me was a baseball bat, with a ball and two gloves.

"We're going to Overton Park," said Trey. "Play a little catch."

I told him where Sun Records was, and he turned the car toward Union. As he drove, he spoke to me over his shoulder.

"Tell me about this place. Do they really record Negroes?"

"Yeah," I said. "I was at a session the other night. There's another one today."

"What's it like to hear them in person?" he asked. "On the radio it sounds so . . . I don't know. Dirty. Mean. Wild. Are they really like that?"

I thought of Pat Hare and his guitar. I thought of the piano player's quiet voice and thoughtful eyes.

"I don't know," I said. "I guess some are. They're just people."

Graydon laughed. "Hear that, Trey? Just people."

Trey stepped on the gas, and we flew down Union Avenue. I leaned back and closed my eyes. A few minutes later we pulled up to Sun. There was no space at the curb, so we went through the alley to the back.

"Thanks for the ride," I said, climbing out.

Trey said, "Oh, there's one more thing."

"What's that?"

"I was at K's Kreem today. K said you called and talked to Ruth Ann."

I looked at Trey. His jaw was set in a hard line. I noticed a scar high on one cheek.

"Well, did you?" he asked.

"I guess so."

"What did you talk about?"

"Nothing much," I said.

"I saw the way you looked at her the other day," he said. "Don't."

"Don't what?"

"Don't look at her. Don't call. Don't talk to her."

I thought of all the times growing up when Trey had pushed me down, held me back, laughed in my face.

I said, "What's your problem?"

"I don't have a problem," he said. "Do you?"

I didn't answer.

He lit up a cigarette, then turned and looked at Sun Records. "So, there's a session this afternoon?"

"That's right," I said.

Trey switched off the engine. "I'd like to see it. I think we'll stay."

I felt panic rising up inside me. "Trey, I just started here. I don't know if they want me bringing people to work."

"Don't worry," said Trey. "It'll be fine."

I heard a car coming up the alley. It was Sam Phillips in his '52 Mercury. He parked and got out, carrying a stack of tape reels under one arm. Something about him seemed to spark and hum, like an electrical generator.

"So, you're back," he said to me. "How come?"

All I could think of was the truth. "I couldn't stay away."

Sam looked over at the Cadillac. "Who are your friends?"

I glanced nervously at Trey and Graydon. "Oh, just a couple of guys I know."

Trey said, "Johnny told us we might be able to sit in on the session today."

"I don't think so," said Sam.

Trey got out of the Cadillac. He held out his hand.

"I'm Trey Chapman. You may know my father—Arthur Chapman?"

"Never met him," said Sam. "Excuse me, I need to go inside." He brushed past Trey and headed for the back door of the studio.

Trey said, "Who are we recording today?"

Sam stopped and stared at him. As he did, another car pulled up the alley. It was a station wagon full of white boys. They parked, opened the back of their car, and began unloading instruments.

"Who are they?" I asked.

"The Starlite Wranglers," said Sam. "That's who we're recording."

Trey groaned. "Man, they're a bunch of hillbillies."

"They're good," said Sam. "That's all that matters."

Trey got back in the Cadillac and started the engine.

"Thanks for the invitation," he told Sam, "but I think we'll be going."

He backed out and tore off down the alley.

"Mr. Phillips, I'm sorry," I said. "I didn't invite them. I wouldn't do that."

"Don't worry about it," he said. "No harm done."

Inside, Sam stacked the reels in the little back room and turned on the tape machine. As he worked, I went into the studio, where Marion Keisker was watching the Starlite Wranglers set up. They were young, probably in their twenties.

When I asked Marion about them, she said, "They're a

country group here in town. That's Clyde Rush on guitar and Millard Yow on pedal steel. Doug Poindexter's a baker, but he thinks he can sing."

Poindexter, a tall man with dark hair, shot her a quick grin. "Now, Miss Marion."

"That fellow with the bass is Bill Black," she went on, gesturing toward a broad-faced man with a big smile. "The guitarist next to him is Scotty Moore, but he desperately wants to be Chet Atkins."

Scotty, a thin man with a baby face and quick, hungry eyes, must have seen that I was confused. "Chet Atkins is the best guitar player in Nashville or pretty much anywhere else," he said. "If you're going to be like somebody, it might as well be him."

As Scotty was talking, Sam entered the room. "I'll tell you who to be like," he said. "There's a fine young guitar player right here in Memphis. Got his own way of playing. His name's Moore. Scotty Moore."

Scotty shook his head. "Aw, Sam."

Sam Phillips looked over and saw me. "If you want to stay, get to work. Grab those music stands and bring them over here."

I did as he asked. As I was moving the stands, he said, "Understand, now, I still can't pay you. You're not an employee."

"What am I?"

"A gofer," said Sam. "You know—gofer this, gofer that. Everybody needs one. God knows, I do."

He turned to the musicians. "What are y'all staring at? Come on, let's make some noise."

They went back to setting up, while Sam fiddled with the microphone.

Marion told me, "Let's go to the control booth. It's right through here."

She led me into the little back room, where we stood next to the tape machine. We watched through the window as the musicians tuned up and played a few practice notes. A moment later Sam joined us. He closed the door to the studio and took his place at the console.

For the next hour they worked on a country song called "My Kind of Carryin' On," with Doug Poindexter doing the vocals and Scotty Moore playing a guitar solo.

Sam listened intently, his eyes closed. Every so often he would stop the group and suggest something. I noticed it usually didn't have anything to do with wrong notes. It was about the song's mood and emotions, what Sam called the "feel." As he worked with them, the unimportant details seemed to fall away, leaving something pure and fine in the center of the song.

Sam had a way of making a song the best it could be. He looked at what was there and tried to see it for what it was, honestly and truthfully. It might not be a great song, or even be a good one. But it was different. It was unique. There was no other song like it. And somewhere, buried deep inside, might be the kernel of something good. If it was there, then Sam would find it.

When they finished the last take, Sam said, "Boys, that'll do it. I believe we've done our best with it."

He went back into the studio to talk with the Starlite Wranglers about the next song. Meanwhile Marion gave me a quick tour of the control booth, showing me each machine and describing what it did. As she was demonstrating the tape player, I heard a door open, and a new voice rang out from the studio.

"Deegaw!"

My back was turned, so I couldn't see who had entered. But there was no mistaking that voice.

Dewey Phillips had arrived.

CHAPTER EIGHT

He was tall and gangly, with curly red hair that flew out at odd angles. He wore a big grin, and his eyes were doing the boogie-woogie. Striding across the studio, he looked as if he had just stepped off a tractor, except instead of overalls he was wearing wrinkled khakis and a Hawaiian shirt. The shirt might have been tucked in that morning, but it had burst free and was flapping loose around his waist.

Puffing on a cigarette, he called out, "Sam, man, didn't anybody tell you it's supper time? You're working these poor boys to death. Ain't that right, boys?"

Doug Poindexter smiled. "Hey, Dewey, how's it hanging?"

Dewey slapped Sam on the back, nearly knocking him over. "Come on, man, I hear a cheeseburger calling my name."

Next to me, Marion smiled and leaned over toward me. "I guess you know who that is."

"I sure do."

Marion led me back into the studio, where Dewey was chatting with Sam and the Starlite Wranglers.

She said, "Don't believe a word he tells you, boys."

Dewey turned around and grinned. "Miss Marion, you brighten up the room like a jar full of lightning bugs."

"Is that a compliment?" she said.

He grabbed her hand and started doing the jitterbug. She joined in, her hair bouncing and her skirt swirling around her knees.

"Where's the music?" asked Scotty.

Dewey tapped the side of his head. "In here, man. In here."

He gave Marion one final twirl. Catching her breath, she smoothed her hair and checked her watch. "My goodness, it's almost six. Sam, can you manage without me?"

"Barely," he said.

Dewey stared at her. "You're leaving, just like that? After dancing with the king of radio?"

Marion pinched his cheek. "You're the king, all right," she said. "King of what I used to shovel in my daddy's cow pasture."

Scotty and the Wranglers laughed at that one, but Dewey didn't mind. "It's true," he said. "Only difference is, I get paid for it."

Marion gave him a hug, said good-bye all around, and left.

"Let's eat," said Dewey, "I'm starving." He bolted for the door, then noticed me for the first time. "Who's he?"

"That's my gofer," said Sam.

Dewey squinted at me, then looked over at Sam.

"You got a gofer? Man, I could use one of them."

Sam said, "Eat your heart out. He's mine."

That made me feel pretty good.

"Has he got a name?" Dewey asked.

"Johnny Ross," I said.

Dewey reached out, and we shook hands. I said, "I like your show."

He shook his head. "Won't be a show if I don't eat. Man, I'm about to dry up and blow away."

I said to Sam, "You all go ahead. I'll straighten up the studio."

Sam said, "Straighten up? You'll mess up the molecules. We got 'em lined up just right. Come on with us."

"Yeah," said Dewey. "Sam might need you to pass the ketchup."

The restaurant next door was a small place—really just a glorified lunch counter with a jukebox, some tables, and a few booths along the windows. The floor was a black-and-white linoleum checkerboard. The stools, chairs, and booths had the same red plastic covering used by every burger joint in town.

The tables were full, so Sam took the first booth and motioned for me to sit beside him. Dewey and Scotty slid in across from us. The other Wranglers got the next booth down. A middle-aged woman wearing an apron came over, holding an order pad and pencil.

"This is Mrs. Dell Taylor," Sam told me. "You do what she says. She owns the joint."

Mrs. Taylor said, "What's a boy like you doing with these people?" I tried to figure out if she was joking, but I couldn't.

"Aw, come on, mama," said Dewey, "give us a smile."
She gazed at him. "I'm not your mama. God help the woman who is."

Dewey said, "I saw Mrs. Taylor smile once. It was in 1942."

"She ain't much fun," said Sam, "but she makes the best burgers in town."

Mrs. Taylor took our orders, then moved on. Dewey jumped up and went over to the jukebox.

Scotty said, "They call this place Mrs. Taylor's, but it's really Sam's office. He signed half his acts right here in this booth."

"I had to," said Sam. "Marion took my desk."

Dewey fired up the jukebox, and the music started. Snapping his fingers over his head, he danced around the floor, calling out, "Deegaw!" The other customers gaped at him. He just grinned.

The song was something called "Rocket 88," about a man, a woman, and a car. It had a rhythm that grabbed hold of you and pushed, hard. Something about it made me want to smile.

Dewey danced back to the booth, flopped down in his seat, and started beating on the table like it was a bongo drum. "Come on, Ike, just flat play it, baby."

Scotty said, "Dewey thinks he's on the radio."

Sam grunted. "He's on something."

"Who's Ike?" I asked.

"Ike Turner," said Scotty. "That's his band on the juke-box. He's playing the piano. 'Rocket 88' was recorded right next door at Sun. Sam sent it to Chess Records in

Chicago. Three months later it was number one on the R&B charts."

Sam said, "Mrs. Taylor didn't want to put it on the jukebox. Said she only wanted country. Finally I talked her into it, and the people loved it. Now she has all my records."

I said, "Could I ask you something?"

"Sure."

"Well, Ike Turner's a Negro, isn't he?" I asked.

Sam nodded.

"Scotty and the Wranglers are white," I said.

"Hey, this kid's sharp," said Dewey.

I didn't know exactly how to say it. "They're so different. Why do you do both?"

Sam's eyebrows bunched up, and his eyes narrowed. There was something behind them, but I couldn't tell what.

"I grew up on a farm in Alabama," he said. "I used to hear Negroes singing in the fields. Heard 'em at church on Sunday. Lord, it was beautiful. There was something real about it. Something honest and true. Most people didn't pay attention, but I did. Still do. When James Cotton sings, the music floats up in the air and then it's gone. I want to grab it and hold it close. Carry it out into the world. Put it in a bottle and sell it. It's why I came to Memphis. Why I started Sun Records."

I glanced over at Scotty. "Then why are you recording the Starlite Wranglers?"

Sam said, "I like country music. I grew up on it."

"He's just a glorified hick," said Dewey. "We all are."

"I don't understand," I said.

Sam heaved a sigh. "Come on, now, don't be like the rest of them. They put white music in one box and black music in another. Like they were different worlds, different planets. It's like Memphis. You got Main Street over here and Beale Street over there. Completely separate, right? But look here. If you go far enough on Main Street, what happens?"

He looked at me, waiting for an answer. "You know Memphis," he said. "What happens?"

I thought about my walks downtown. I pictured Main Street, up by the Gayoso Hotel. Walk north and you see Ellis Auditorium. Walk south . . .

"They cross," I said.

He slapped his hand on the table. "That's right. It's a geographical fact. People don't want to think about it, but it's true. Main Street crosses Beale Street. And you know what? It's the most interesting corner in town."

Mrs. Taylor approached the table, with plates of burgers stacked up and down her arms.

"Look at that," said Dewey. "Ain't she the most beautiful thing you ever saw?"

"Eat your heart out," said Mrs. Taylor, never cracking a smile. She handed out the burgers, then pulled a ketchup bottle from her apron pocket and set it on the table.

Dewey noticed the ketchup bottle and nodded to me. "All right, now, do your job."

I picked up the bottle and passed it to Sam. Dewey shook his head in admiration. "A gofer," he said. "Man, I got to get me one of them."

Mrs. Taylor was back a minute later with milk shakes and fries.

She said, "If you want something else, just holler."

"And what would you do?" asked Dewey.

"I'd holler right back," she said.

We dug in. For a few minutes the only sounds were the buzz of the customers, the clattering of dishes, and music from the jukebox. Dewey must have been starving, just like he had said, because by the time I looked up from my burger, his was gone. He finished off his milk shake, and when he glanced around for something to do, he saw salt and pepper shakers by the napkin dispenser. He grabbed the salt and set it on the table in front of him.

"All right, now, here's the way I see it," Dewey told me. "I like salt. It's white, but the flavor's good. It makes things taste better."

He picked up the pepper shaker and set it next to the salt. "I like pepper, too. It adds spice. It's black, but not pure black. It's got punch. It's got zip. It makes life interesting. Ain't that right, Sam?"

Sam thought about it for a minute. He picked up the salt and shook some out on the table. Then sprinkled some pepper next to it.

"I like salt and pepper too," he said. "Both of them are good in their own way. But here's what I really like."

He reached out with his finger and swirled the salt and pepper together. "Salt and pepper mixed together. Lots of flavor, lots of spice. Not white. Not black. Something in between."

"Tell 'em, Sam," said Scotty.

"Aw, hush," he said.

"Come on, tell him."

Sam said, "If you know so much about it, you tell him."

"All right, I will," said Scotty. "Sam and me, we like to drop by Mrs. Taylor's and have a cup of coffee. We talk about country music and gospel and the blues. Sometimes we talk about Sun Records and what comes next. Now, Sam's doing okay. He's recorded for other labels, and he's had a few hits of his own. But he has an idea that could be bigger than all that."

Sam had been fidgeting while Scotty talked. His eyes were darting back and forth, and finally he couldn't sit still any longer. He jumped up from the booth and paced back and forth next to it.

"Hey, Sam, you okay?" asked Dewey.

Sam didn't answer.

Dewey said, "He's like that sometimes. Sam, man, you there?"

Sam stopped pacing. He placed his palms on the table and leaned in close to me. His breath smelled like onions. His eyes were on fire.

"You heard that record? 'Rocket 88'?"

"Yes, sir."

"Did you like it?"

"Yes, I did."

"Would you buy it?"

"I'm not sure where they sell it," I said. "And if I bought it, well . . ."

I wanted to tell the truth, but it was embarrassing.

"Come on," said Sam. "Be honest, now."

"Well, I don't know what my mother would think."

"Exactly!" he said. He turned to the others. "There's white kids all over town who liked that record. They heard it on the radio, probably on your show, Dewey. But they didn't buy it. You know why?"

Dewey looked away. Scotty shifted uncomfortably.

"I'll tell you," said Sam. "It pains me to say it. I hate that it's true. But it's a fact. They didn't buy it because it was sung by a Negro."

I noticed that all of a sudden the room was quiet. A woman cleared her throat. A man ducked his head, reaching into his pocket for change. An older couple stared at Sam, jaws set, like he'd done something bad, like he'd stepped over an invisible line.

It didn't bother Sam. He stared right back at them, and they looked away. Turning toward us, he leaned in close and said, "There's a way around it, you know. A way to make the whole thing work. What you need is black music. But you don't get a Negro to sing it. Right, Scotty?"

Scotty nodded. "That's right."

"Who do you get?" asked Dewey.

Sam said, "You get a white boy."

Dewey burst out laughing. "Oh, yeah. Right. Get a white boy. Only one problem."

"What's that?" asked Sam.

"It wouldn't work. He wouldn't be any good. Man, you might as well ask my dog to smoke a cigar."

"You don't have a dog," said Scotty.

"What about Bill Haley?" asked Sam.

I glanced over at Scotty. He explained, "Bill Haley's a

singer back east. He does songs that are supposed to sound like R&B—you know, Negro music. He did 'Crazy, Man, Crazy' and 'Rock Around the Clock.' He's white."

"Not just white," said Dewey. "He's pale. He's blanched. He's arctic. Man, have you heard him? Sings like his pants are all bunched up."

"Didn't he do a version of 'Rocket 88'?" asked Scotty.

Dewey nodded. "They wanted me to play it on my show. I said, 'How can I play that and ever look Ike Turner in the face?'"

"Yeah," said Sam, "but they sold a lot of records."

Dewey said, "They sell a lot of toilet paper, too, but that doesn't mean I want to help."

"You don't understand," said Sam. "I don't want somebody who sounds white, like Bill Haley. I want him to sound black."

"A white singer who sounds black?" said Dewey. "Good luck."

Sam leaned back and crossed his arms. "If I could find a white boy who sang like a Negro, I'd make me a million dollars."

Dewey stared at Sam. "Lord, I think he's serious."

"And I'm going to find him," said Sam.

We finished our burgers and went back to the studio. The Starlite Wranglers worked on another song, with me and Dewey in the control booth looking over Sam's shoulder. Dewey left after that, and I stayed around to clean up.

It was late when I got home that night. My mother was asleep. I got a glass of ice water in the kitchen, then went to my room and climbed in bed. Reaching over, I turned on the radio.

"Deegaw!" said Dewey Phillips.

He was talking to all of Memphis, but just a few hours earlier he had been talking to me. I settled back and listened, feeling like I was in the center of the world.

CHAPTER NINE

"They caught 'em!" said Lamont.

"Caught who?" I asked.

"Those boys who burned the cross. It was in the morning paper. Take a look."

It was Saturday morning. I had woken up to find my mother by herself in the living room, eyes closed, dancing to the music of Doris Day.

"So it's true," I told her. "You really can dance."

She opened her eyes and switched off the record player. "Where were you last night?"

I thought back to the day at Sun Records, supper at Mrs. Taylor's, and the late-night recording session. It had all happened so fast I'd forgotten to tell my mother.

"Sorry," I said. "I should have called."

"I was worried sick. What were you doing?"

For a moment I wondered if a part of her would understand where I'd been, the part that had danced at the

Peabody and had fun. Then I pushed the thought aside. Sun Records was mine. I didn't want her to know about it, and I certainly didn't want her telling me not to go.

I shrugged. "I was at a friend's house. I'm sorry, Mom. Next time I'll call. I promise."

"You'd better," she said.

She left to run some errands, and I wandered out to the curb. A few minutes later, Lamont pulled up in his blue Ford, flashing the newspaper. He handed it to me, and I read about the arrest of the cross burners.

"They'll have a hearing in a couple of weeks," said Lamont. "Maybe there's justice after all—even in Memphis."

He shot me a grin. "You know, it was the license number that did it."

"Really?"

He gestured toward the article. "That's what it says. See here? 'Two concerned citizens.' That's you and me."

I scanned the article. It quoted Officer Linebaugh, the man I'd spoken to at the police station. I told Lamont about my visit there and the way I'd been treated. Lamont wasn't surprised.

"Hey, man, that's what happens when you're with a Negro."

"You think so?"

"Where have you been? That's the way things work. And look here. They sent the Negro officer back to the projects, like he couldn't handle it. Then the white cop got all the credit."

"That's not right," I said.

"Turns out my father knows Officer Barnes, the Negro cop. Barnes told him what we did. My father didn't like it. Said I shouldn't be driving around late at night, especially with no white boy."

"Your father sounds like my mom," I said.

"He told me to stop spending time with you," said Lamont.

"Oh, yeah? Then why are you here?"

Lamont grinned. "That's why I'm here."

I laughed. Lamont said, "You know, I'm supposed to be with my father right now. He and my mother have an agreement. I spend Saturdays with him. Only trouble is, nobody asked me."

"What are you going to do?"

"I'm not sure," he said. Then his expression brightened. "Hey, maybe you could come with me. I wonder what he'd say."

"Come with you? Where?"

"To my father's house."

"Will has a house?"

Something in his face changed, and I knew I'd made a mistake. He said, "Yeah. Something wrong with that?"

"I mean, where does he live?"

"You want to come or not?" asked Lamont.

I had a feeling his question was another test. It seemed that, for Lamont, life was full of tests. They never ended. They just went on and on.

I wondered what my mother would say. I knew she'd be upset. Maybe that's what finally convinced me.

"Sure," I said. "Let's go."

Using his left hand to spin the steering wheel, he did a U-turn and headed west on Union, then north on Manassas Street. Up ahead I saw a big brick building with concrete towers on the roof. It was Humes High, the school where Elvis had gone.

Lamont turned onto a side street. As I looked around, I thought of how different the neighborhood was from where I lived. Cars were parked in front of the houses, something that rarely happened on Belvedere Boulevard. A boy my age, probably a student at Humes High, had a hose and bucket and was washing an old Chevy. There was a bicycle on one lawn and a red wagon on another. Kids were playing.

We turned a corner and went down another block. It was like the first one, with one big difference. Suddenly, as if someone had flipped a switch, all the people were Negroes. The picture was the same, with the cars and bicycles and kids playing in the grass, but now the faces were black instead of white. A teenage girl sat on the steps of one house. Though she lived only a few blocks from Humes High, I knew she didn't go there. She took a bus to a school on the other side of town.

Halfway down the block was a small, well-kept bungalow. Lamont pulled up to the curb, and we got out. There was a flower bed in front, dotted with daisies. On the porch was a rocking chair and a swing. A cat lay on the swing, stretching. I followed Lamont to the porch, where he knocked on the screen door.

"Just a minute," someone called.

A short time later, Will appeared. He looked different,

and for a moment I couldn't figure out why. Then I realized what it was. He wasn't wearing a uniform. When he worked around the Chapmans' house, he had on a khaki shirt and pants. When he was driving, he wore a chauffeur's suit and cap.

Today he wore some old slacks with frayed cuffs and a pair of comfortable-looking moccasins. His short-sleeved shirt was unbuttoned, showing an undershirt beneath. He carried a glass with an inch of golden liquid in it.

"Well, it's about time," he said to Lamont. Then he saw me. "What are you doing here?"

"I asked him to come," said Lamont.

Will said, "Shouldn't have done that, boy."

"Why not?"

"It's dangerous."

Lamont stared at him. "Man, what are you talking about?"

"Don't call me man," said Will.

"Don't call me boy," said Lamont.

They stood there, staring at each other, like mirror images. I saw that now. The family resemblance was in their anger.

Lamont said, "You want me, you get him, too."

Will glanced at the street to see if anyone was watching, then held open the door.

"Get inside," he said. "Both of you."

CHAPTER TEN

Lamont stepped inside, and I followed. Will closed the door behind us.

In the living room was an African rug of vivid red and green. There was a fireplace and a row of vases lined up on the mantel, each holding a flower. A newspaper was folded neatly on the leather sofa.

"This is nice," I said.

"Are you surprised?" asked Lamont.

"No."

"Some people would be," he said. "Like Trey Chapman."

"Trey Chapman's a fool," said Will.

"Why don't you tell him that?" asked Lamont.

"Listen here," said Will. "There's two different things—what you say to white people, and the truth. Don't ever get them confused."

"It shouldn't be that way," said Lamont.

"But it is."

"What about me?" I said. "I'm white."

Will took a sip from his glass, watching me.

"There's iced tea in the fridge," he said.

When he headed for the kitchen, I saw some pictures on the wall and went over to look at them. They were old black-and-white photographs showing a Negro family posed stiffly, with serious expressions. They reminded me of some we had at my house; in fact, the photos could have been negatives of ours, with black faces instead of white.

On the top row was a larger, framed portrait of a stern-looking woman with her hair in a bun. I recognized her as the teenage girl in the family picture.

Will came back from the kitchen. He handed each of us a glass of iced tea.

"Who's that woman?" I asked.

"Hattie Mae Johnson," he said. "She was my mother."

It was obvious if you looked for it. She had the same nose and mouth as Will, and her eyes, even in the photo, bore into you the way his did sometimes. Her skin was lighter than his by a couple of shades. If you saw her on the street, it might have been hard to tell that she was a Negro. There was something familiar about her.

"Did I ever meet her?" I asked.

He shook his head. "She died two years after that picture was taken. She lived a hard life."

"What did she do?"

"All kinds of things. Domestic work mostly. In her spare time she raised five children."

I said, "What about your father?"

"What about him?"

"Do you have a picture?" I asked.

"He left before I came along."

"Yours too, huh?"

He gave me a long, searching look. Finally he said, "Yeah, mine too."

It occurred to me that I knew almost nothing about Will. Usually he didn't like questions. Today, with a drink in his hand, things might be different.

"How did you meet Mr. Chapman?" I asked.

"I saw an ad in the paper. He was looking for a handyman. I've been working for him ever since."

"Was my father with him then?"

Will nodded. "Your mother, too. She was the first. Chapman was having trouble with one of his cars, and she said her husband could fix it. Pretty soon he was driving Chapman around town. Chapman fixed up the little house in back for them to live in, so his driver would always be close by."

"Why did he leave?"

Certain questions were discouraged at my house, and that was one of them. Maybe my mother thought that not talking about it would stop me from thinking about it.

Will swirled his drink. "Who knows why a man does things."

"Maybe he didn't want children," I said.

"Maybe."

I said, "Sometimes I wonder why Mr. Chapman let my mother stay in the house after my father left."

"He was afraid if she left the house, she might leave, period."

"You mean, he liked her?"

He gazed at me, as if deciding what to say. Finally he looked down. "No, man. She did his books, that's all."

Will picked up a bottle and poured himself another drink. Lamont wandered over to the radio. He twisted a dial, and music filled the room. It was a slow blues number, sung by a woman with a gravelly voice. The music ended, and a man spoke.

"*Well, yessiree, it's Nat D., coming to thee at seventy-three, WDIA. Now, whatchubet?*" He gave a big, hearty laugh. Another song started, this one an up-tempo number like the one I'd heard Lamont play at the club.

Will said, "That's WDIA right here in Memphis. First all-Negro station in the country."

"Is that Nat D. Williams?" I asked.

Will cocked his head. "You know who he is?"

"Tuesday night I went to Beale Street. I ended up at the Palace Theater."

Will said to Lamont, "You took him to Beale Street?"

"I went on my own," I said.

Will stared at me. The lines in his forehead got deeper, like furrows in the soil. Then something seemed to burst loose. He laughed and shook his head. "Lord have mercy. Johnny Ross at amateur night."

"Don't tell my mother, okay?"

"Wouldn't dream of it."

I said, "Do you know Nat D. Williams?"

"Everybody knows Nat D. If Memphis had a mayor of

Negroes, he'd be it. Host of amateur night. Emcee of the Cotton Makers' Jubilee. Newspaper column. Radio show. Course, that's just on the side. His real job is teaching social studies at Booker T. Washington High School."

"He's a teacher?"

"The best," said Will. "Before I started with Mr. Chapman, I was a janitor there. You might say he took me under his wing. On Friday afternoons I'd make a point of sweeping the hall outside his class. If he was in a good mood, he'd close the books and talk about Beale Street. He was born there, you know. Goes back every chance he gets. The King of Beale Street—that's what they call him."

Talking about amateur night reminded me of Elvis Presley and my trip to Sun Records. I told them about going there and seeing the recording session.

Lamont said, "What did you think of Pat Hare?"

"He made me nervous," I said.

Lamont shook his head. "White people see a Negro, they think he's going to pull a knife on them. Well, that's just crazy—unless it's Pat Hare. He'd do it. But he can sure play."

"So can you," I said.

Will said, "You heard Lamont?"

I told him about my trip to the Grey Mule. Lamont said to Will, "You should come down there sometime."

I said, "He hasn't heard you?"

"No, man, he's too busy."

"You should come down *here* sometime," said Will. "You're supposed to spend Saturdays with me."

There was an uncomfortable silence. I asked Lamont, "Have you ever made a record?"

"No."

"I could introduce you to Sam Phillips. He owns Sun Records."

"I know who he is. I see him down on Beale, poking around, talking to people. Just another white man making money off Negroes."

"That's not the way it is," I said.

"That's always the way it is."

The music played on the radio. It was another slow blues tune. When the song ended, Nat D. Williams jumped in.

"Remember, folks, tomorrow's the Fourth of July. Big doings on Beale. Come on down after church. Lots of barbecue. Lots of music."

Lamont perked up. "Sounds good. You want to go, Johnny?"

Will glared at him. Lamont glared right back.

"Sorry," I said. "I'm meeting a friend at St. Peter's."

Lamont looked at me, puzzled.

I said, "It's an orphanage. They have a big Fourth of July picnic every year to raise money."

"Maybe I'll go," said Lamont.

Will said, "Forget it."

"Why?" asked Lamont.

"The only Negroes there will be serving food and picking up trash. It's for white folks."

The Fourth of July was Independence Day, when we celebrated our freedom. I thought about Negroes having their own party on Beale Street and wondered how they felt about it.

"It's not fair," said Lamont. "Johnny came here. Why can't I go there?"

"Boy," muttered Will, "you got a lot to learn."

We spent the next few hours listening to music. Lamont knew the names of all the musicians. He'd even met some of them. He told us what they were like and what he thought about their music. Finally, late in the afternoon, I looked at my watch.

"I'd better be going," I said. I didn't want my mother to worry. The last thing I needed was her asking me questions about where I'd been.

Lamont nodded. "I'll drive you home."

"No, you won't," said Will. He took some coins from his pocket and handed them to me. "Number three bus. Transfer at Union."

Lamont said, "Hey, man—"

Will's eyes flashed. "Just do as I say."

Lamont stared at him for a long time. Then he dropped his gaze and headed for the door. "See you around, Johnny," he said.

I watched him walk to his car, then looked at Will. "I don't understand."

"One of these days you will."

"Is it really dangerous?" I asked.

"You have no idea," he said.

It had been hot for days, and the Fourth of July was no different. My mother and I went to a parade in the morning, then came back home for lunch. Toward the end of the afternoon I headed over to St. Peter's Orphanage. It seemed like half of Memphis was there. After talking to Will, I now realized which half.

The orphanage had a huge lawn, and that day it was swarming with people. There were game booths and carnival rides. Vendors roamed through the crowd, selling hot dogs, cotton candy, and lemonade.

A few days before, when Trey had asked about my phone call to Ruth Ann, I hadn't told him the reason for my call. I had invited Ruth Ann to St. Peter's for the picnic. She said she would be working at the bottle-toss booth and suggested that I drop by. It wasn't exactly a date, but it was close enough for me. The only problem was that Trey beat me to it.

He stood at the booth, holding a tennis ball, with kids lined up behind him. Inside was Ruth Ann, setting up the bottles, with her hair pinned up to keep it out of her eyes. I wondered what her hair felt like. I wanted to touch it, to see if it was as soft as it looked.

I remembered the way Trey had held her at K's. Every time I thought about it, my stomach tightened. Sure, I told myself, she liked him. But he wasn't really interested in her. He just wanted to show her off, like his fancy clothes or his Cadillac. I was certain she would figure that out. Maybe she already knew. After all, when I'd asked her out she had said yes. Or at least, she hadn't said no. That was the important thing.

Trey eyed the bottles and took aim. Then he reared back, set his big shoulders, and whipped the ball into the booth with such speed that I could barely see it. The bottles exploded into the air, then came crashing down like tenpins in a bowling alley.

"That was the last one, okay?" said Ruth Ann. "Let's give the kids a chance."

"Are you kidding?" said Trey. "I'm just getting warmed up."

Ruth Ann set up the bottles and handed Trey another ball. He fired it again. This time the ball hit the edge of the table and went rocketing right back toward Ruth Ann, hitting her in the head. Her hands flew to her face, and she doubled over at the waist. Without thinking, I hopped over the barrier into the booth.

Trey glared at me. "What are you doing here?"

"Are you all right?" I asked Ruth Ann. Straightening up, she took her hands from her face. There was a bright red spot high on one cheek.

"I think so," she said.

"Get away from her," said Trey, who had jumped the barrier and was looming over me.

"What are you trying to prove?" I said. "It's not war. It's a game."

Trey shoved me aside and peered at Ruth Ann's face. "You're okay, right?"

She nodded. Trey put his arm around her.

"Let's get out of here," he said. "My family's having a picnic tonight. It's a lot better than this."

She shook her head. "I can't, Trey. I promised I'd work at the booth."

"Aw, come on."

"You go ahead. I'll see you tomorrow."

He leaned over and kissed her. As he turned back, he noticed me again.

"I told you to stay away," he said.

"I was just walking by."

"Get out of here."

I glanced at Ruth Ann, who was watching me as she picked up the bottles. She turned to the group of kids waiting in line.

"Okay, who's next?" she said.

I took one last look at her, then left. Wandering through the crowd, I watched the people, but all I saw was Ruth Ann. Twenty minutes later, I found myself back at the booth. The line was gone. Ruth Ann had her back turned, setting up the bottles. An older woman was in the booth with her.

"Want to give it a try?" the woman asked me.

"You might say that," I replied.

Ruth Ann, hearing my voice, turned around. She smiled, and our eyes met. The woman watched us.

"Would you like to leave?" she asked Ruth Ann. "I can handle things here."

"Really? Is that okay?"

"You go ahead, dear. Have fun."

Ruth Ann got her purse from the back and came out to join me.

"What do you think?" she asked, displaying a red, white, and blue skirt. "Am I patriotic enough?"

"It's beautiful," I said. She could have been wearing dirty overalls and I would have said the same thing.

She took my hand. I glanced around nervously.

"Trey's gone," she said. "He went to his family picnic."

Yes, I thought, but his friends didn't.

She said, "Sometimes he makes me mad. He doesn't own me."

"I've known him a long time," I said. "He's used to getting what he wants."

"Him and his money. It's all he ever talks about."

"You won't have that problem with me," I said.

She smiled and squeezed my hand. We set off, moving through the crowd.

As we walked, she told me about her summer. She talked about church activities and working at K's. I noticed she didn't mention Trey again. I decided that was a good sign.

I guess I was still nervous, though, because when there was a popping noise behind us, I jumped.

Ruth Ann laughed. "That was a balloon, silly. It's the dart-throwing booth."

I looked at it, trying to act as if I'd known all along. The balloons were fastened to a board, and on the shelf above it was a row of teddy bears.

Pointing to the teddy bears, I said, "Would you like one?"

"Oh, Johnny, you don't have to do that."

"I want to," I said. "I'll win one for you."

I pulled a nickel from my pocket and handed it to the attendant, who gave me three darts. As Ruth Ann watched, I popped three balloons in a row. For once, everything seemed to be going my way.

"Here you are, sir," said the attendant. He handed me a teddy bear. Grinning proudly, I passed it to Ruth Ann.

"Thank you," she said. "That's very sweet."

She gave the teddy bear a hug. I swear I could feel it.

Behind me someone said, "Well, if it isn't Johnny Ross."

Turning around, I saw Marion Keisker. She was holding the hand of a little girl who had pigtails tied up with bright red ribbons.

Marion said, "Looks like you got a prize. And I don't mean the teddy bear."

"This is Ruth Ann Morris," I said, blushing. "She's a friend of mine."

Marion smiled. "I'm Marion Keisker. This is my niece, Emily."

Ruth Ann bent down to Emily's level. "Are you having fun?" she asked.

Emily nodded and said, "That's a nice teddy bear."

"Would you like it?" asked Ruth Ann.

"Oh, yes!"

Ruth Ann handed her the teddy bear. I have to admit, it made me sad. It also made me wonder. Giving Emily the teddy bear was a nice gesture. It was also a way to make sure Trey never saw it.

Saying good-bye to Marion and Emily, we headed for the food booths. We got some fried chicken and potato salad and found a spot at a picnic table. As we ate, I found myself telling Ruth Ann about Marion and Sam and Sun Records. Usually I had trouble talking to girls, but somehow that night it was easy. Ruth Ann listened, nodding and asking questions. It could have been my imagination, but I thought she might be looking at me in a different way—with respect, maybe even admiration.

Later, when the sky turned dark, we bought some ice-cream cones, found a spot on the lawn, and settled in to wait for the big event. Everybody liked the food and games at St. Peter's, but what they really looked forward to was the fireworks. It was the best show of the year, and you could see it for miles around.

A man stepped up to the microphone. "Folks," he said, "I have an announcement. Today's the Fourth of July, but it's also Sunday. The picnic committee felt that, being the Lord's day and all, it wouldn't be right to have a fireworks show."

The crowd groaned. I looked at Ruth Ann and shrugged. She smiled.

The man held up his hand. "Now, you'll notice I didn't say the fireworks show was canceled. It's just postponed. Come back tomorrow night, same time and place, and we'll give you the best show you've ever seen. Sorry about this, folks. We hope you'll understand."

The crowd started to wander off. Ruth Ann and I stayed, finishing up our cones. A full moon rose over the trees. I thought about all the things that had happened over the past two weeks—seeing Ruth Ann, going to Beale Street, meeting Elvis, riding with Lamont, finding Sun Records.

Ruth Ann finished the last of her cone and put her head on my shoulder. I pressed my cheek against her hair. She pulled away for a moment, looking up at me. Then she leaned in and placed her lips against mine. I kissed her. Her lips tasted like strawberry ice cream.

Beyond the trees, there was music. A man was singing with a dance band. I recognized a Frank Sinatra song from the year before: *Fairy tales can come true, it can happen to you if you're young at heart . . .*

Something was happening in Memphis. It was happening to me. There was a feeling in the air, beginning to form. Like the fireworks, it was ready to explode, but it hadn't happened yet. I looked up at the sky, waiting.

PART 2

WHITE

The gypsy woman told my mother
Before I was born
I got a boy child's comin'
He's gonna be a son of a gun
He gonna make pretty womens
Jump and shout
Then the world wanna know
What this all about

        —Muddy Waters

CHAPTER ELEVEN

Sam burst into the studio.

"Come on, boy," he said, "I'm not paying you to sleep."

"You're not paying me at all," I said drowsily. I had been cleaning and must have nodded off.

"Pick up those boxes," he said. "While you're at it, throw away the Coke bottles and candy wrappers. We got a session tonight."

It was late the next day. The night before, Ruth Ann and I had made the rounds of every booth at St. Peter's, then taken the bus home, holding hands and gazing out into the darkness. After getting home I was too excited to sleep, so I tuned my radio to WDIA, the all-Negro station, and listened into the early morning hours.

I had slept until lunchtime but was still groggy when I woke up. Later that afternoon my mother had come home from work with a bag of groceries, only to find me heading out the door.

"Where are you going?" she had asked.

I still hadn't told her about Sun Records. Thinking quickly, I said, "I met a friend at Poplar Tunes. He invited me to eat at his place."

"You could have called and told me. I was planning to make a casserole."

"Sorry," I said.

"Who's this friend? It's not Lamont Turner, is it?"

"No, it's just a friend. Look, I have to go."

When I got to Sun, Marion had already gone home and Sam was busy in the control booth. I worked for a while in the studio, then sat down and had been dozing until Sam had interrupted me.

Reaching for a broom, I stifled a yawn. "What's the session?" I asked.

"It's an audition," he said. "A singer. Scotty and Bill are backing him up."

Scotty and Bill arrived a few minutes later and started setting up. As they did, they talked about a rehearsal with the singer at Scotty's house the night before.

"How was he?" asked Sam.

Scotty shrugged. "The boy's got a good voice, but he doesn't know how to use it. He didn't really knock me out."

Sam said, "Well, let's see how it goes."

I went to the front room to get some things while Sam and the others finished setting up. While I was there, the door opened, and someone peered inside. It was Elvis Presley.

"Come on in," I said. "There's a session in a few minutes. Maybe you could stay and listen."

Elvis shot me a weak smile. "I know there's a session. It's me."

I stared at him. "You're the singer?"

"Mr. Phillips asked me to come."

Elvis stepped inside, carrying a guitar case that looked like he had bought it at Schwab's Drugs. He was dressed in pink and black, like before, with the same two-toned shoes. When he reached up to push the hair out of his eyes, I noticed that his hand was shaking and his face was white.

"Are you nervous?" I asked.

"Naw. I done this before."

I went back into the studio, and Elvis followed me. "Your singer's here," I said, nice and loud so they'd notice.

Scotty looked up at me. "What are you, the receptionist?"

"I like Marion better," said Bill.

Sam came striding across the studio, smiling. He shook Elvis's hand. "How's it goin', Elvis?"

"All right, I reckon."

Sam said, "We're gonna make some music tonight. Right, boys?"

"Yes, sir," said Scotty.

"They were just telling me about last night," said Sam. "I hear you sounded good."

"Thank you," said Elvis. He didn't seem to know what to do with his hands, and his knee was jiggling.

Sam said, "We're all set up. You want a Coke?"

Elvis shook his head. Catching sight of the microphone, he moved across the room, as if drawn by a magnet.

"That's a Shure," said Sam. "Best microphone money can buy."

Elvis gazed at it, a dreamy look on his face. I had the feeling you could throw the microphone over a cliff and he would jump right after it.

Sam made some adjustments to it, talking to Elvis as he worked. Elvis said he had been born in Tupelo, just a few miles down the road in Mississippi. They had moved to Memphis when he was thirteen. He didn't say much about his father, but his mother worked at St. Joseph's Hospital.

After a while, Elvis opened his case and pulled out a guitar. It was a kid's model, smaller than the one Scotty had. Elvis had obviously been getting some use out of it, though, because it was covered with dents and scratches. He strummed a few chords, then tuned up with Scotty and Bill.

Sam, watching him, seemed satisfied. He asked what Elvis wanted to sing, and they discussed it for a few minutes. Sam steered him toward slow ballads. He suggested "Harbor Lights," a Bing Crosby tune, and they decided to give it a try.

"All right, boys, let's do it," said Sam.

He motioned to me, and we went into the control booth. Sam pushed a couple of buttons. A red light came on, and the tape reels started turning. He said into the microphone, "Rolling."

Scotty started with a solo, then Elvis came in. Sometimes it was like he was singing through his nose. Other times it came from deep in his chest. I tried to figure out what his voice sounded like, but I couldn't. One thing for sure: It was different. And that's what Sam wanted. He had told me he was always looking for something new, something he had never heard before.

Next they tried "I Love You Because," a slow song I had heard on the radio. Sam tried to help Elvis relax, but with each new take I could see him getting more worried. His knee jiggled. His eyes darted around the room. A whiny sound began creeping into his voice.

I looked up at the clock and was surprised to see that it was almost nine. Sam must have noticed the same thing, because he opened the door to the studio and suggested they take a break. Scotty and Bill put down their instruments. Sam stayed in the control booth, adjusting one of the machines. I was watching him, when all of a sudden I heard Elvis singing. This time it wasn't a ballad. It was something fast and easy, with a beat that he strummed on his guitar: *"Well, that's all right, mama, that's all right for you."*

Bill picked up his bass and started playing along, then Scotty joined in. Sam stopped what he was doing and stared through the window into the studio, his eyes as big as silver dollars. Next thing I knew, he was across the room, sticking his head out the door. I don't think I had ever seen anyone move quite so fast.

"What are you doing?" he asked them.

"We don't know," said Scotty.

Sam said, "Well, back up, find a place to start, and do it again." He closed the door and turned to me.

"Good Lord, son, you know what that is? It's a blues song. Big Boy Crudup wrote it. Where did he ever learn that?"

I said, "Probably on Beale Street. He's down there all the time."

Sam's eyebrows shot up. "He is? Well, what do you know."

He moved back to the console, leaned into the microphone, and said, "All right, boys. From the top. Let's have some fun."

Sam pressed a couple of buttons, and they started again. Elvis strummed. Bill slapped his bass. Scotty's guitar wove in and out, playing a phrase here, a chord there. There were just three of them, but suddenly, instead of separate instruments, they were a band.

As for the voice, it was as if a different singer had walked into the studio. This one was older. He was loose and confident. He still ranged up and down, but there was no straining on the high notes, and the whine was gone. As he sang, he grinned at the others, and they grinned back.

"Whoo-ee!" said Sam. "Just listen to 'em."

There were some mistakes and a few rough spots, but that didn't bother Sam. In between takes he talked about the feel of the music—what it was and what it wanted to be. He told Scotty, "Man, that's too complicated. Simplify! Let it breathe."

I thought about the blues I had heard on Beale Street. This was similar, but it was different, too. It was lighter. Some of the edges had been rounded off. But the music was still there, riding on the voice of Elvis Presley.

They did take after take, but it was no longer work. Each time it got simpler, freer, more relaxed. By the final take, Sam thought they had something. He called them into the control booth and played it back for them.

"Is that us?" said Bill.

Scotty chuckled nervously. "It sure sounds different."

Sam said, "It's not black. It's not white. It's not gospel. It's not hillbilly."

"So, what is it?" asked Scotty.

"It's something new," said Sam.

They looked over at Elvis. He gave a little half smile, drumming his fingers absently on the wall. He was far away, hearing the music, singing along.

For some reason I thought of Will Turner. Will had said the world was dangerous. Listening to Elvis, I thought I could hear the danger. But it didn't scare me the way it seemed to frighten Will. It was exciting. It was thrilling. It made me feel strong and reckless.

Outside, there was a rumbling sound, then a series of explosions. Scotty hurried to the back door, and we followed him into the alley. Above the roof, the sky was filled with color—red, blue, brilliant white. Independence Day was over, but the fireworks had just started.

CHAPTER TWELVE

"Get ready, Dewey," said Sam. "Here it comes."

Sam started the machine, and the voice of Elvis Presley jumped through the speakers, singing "That's All Right, Mama."

It was Thursday afternoon. For the past few days Sam had been holed up in the studio with Elvis, Scotty, and Bill, trying to recapture the magic of Monday night. It hadn't worked. Finally he sent them home and called Dewey Phillips. I stuck around to see what would happen.

Now Dewey sat in the control booth, a bottle of beer in his hand, listening. When the song ended, Sam said, "What do you think?"

Dewey took a swallow of beer. "At first I thought he must be a Negro. But he's not."

"No, he's not," said Sam.

"It's a blues song by Big Boy Crudup. But it doesn't sound like the blues."

Sam said, "It's different from anything I've ever heard. I can't describe it. I can't put it in a box. I just keep listening. Every time, I love it a little bit more."

Dewey asked about the singer and the session. They sat there for the longest time, playing the song and discussing it. Finally Dewey got to his feet.

"I'd like to say it's a hit, but I'm not sure." he said. "Tell you what, though. I'll play it on my show tonight. We'll let the people decide."

Sam clapped him on the back, spilling Dewey's beer. While I cleaned it up, they walked to Dewey's car, talking excitedly. When Sam came back in, he cut a couple of acetates, which could be used for masters or played on a phonograph, like a record.

We took the acetates to the Hotel Chisca down on Main, where Dewey would be doing his show later that night, then headed off to tell Elvis the news. Elvis lived with his mother, father, and grandmother in a house on Alabama Avenue, not far from the hospital where his mother worked. They had just finished supper when we got there.

Elvis introduced us to his parents, Gladys and Vernon, and his grandmother, Minnie. Gladys and Vernon were clearing the dishes. I noticed that Elvis didn't touch his.

Watching his parents, I was surprised at how ordinary they looked. Gladys was a little plump, with dark hair and a pretty smile. Vernon had a square jaw and was graying around the temples. Next to them, Elvis wore a shirt that was so bright, you could barely look at it without squinting. The three of them made a strange group, as if a couple of sparrows had given birth to a peacock.

Sam turned to Elvis. "Better warm up your radio, son," he said. "It looks like Dewey Phillips is going to play your song on his show tonight."

Elvis said, "Dewey Phillips? *Red Hot and Blue?*"

Sam nodded. Gladys let out a shriek and threw her arms around Elvis. He smiled shyly. Vernon gave him an awkward pat on the shoulder.

Gladys pumped Sam for more information. He told her what he could, then said he had to be going.

Elvis turned to me. "I think I'll go to a movie tonight. Want to come?"

"What about the radio show?" I asked.

"I'm not going to listen," said Elvis. "Too nervous."

Gladys patted his arm. "That's all right. Your father and I will."

"Come on, Johnny," said Elvis. "I've got the car. Let's get out of here."

I was already running late for supper, and I didn't want to lie to my mother again. But I wanted to go with Elvis. Seeing the shy smile on his face, it occurred to me that maybe he needed a friend. And that gave me an idea.

"Okay," I said, "but let's stop by my house on the way."

When we got there, I heard my mother in the kitchen.

"Supper's ready," she called. "Go wash your hands, Johnny."

We went to the kitchen and stood in the doorway. I watched my mother when she turned around. Her eyes got kind of wide, and I could see why. Elvis was wearing one of his Lansky Brothers outfits, with pink stripes.

"Mom," I said, "this is the friend I've been telling you about. His name is Elvis Presley."

She wiped off her hands and extended one to Elvis. "Pleased to meet you, Elvis. Can you stay for supper?"

"Sorry," I said quickly, "but we already ate."

She eyed me sternly. "Now, Johnny, I hope you didn't have supper with the Presleys again."

Elvis shot me a puzzled look. I said, "No, I didn't." At least that much was true.

"We're going to the picture show," said Elvis.

"I wanted to come by first so you could meet him," I added.

My mother eyed Elvis. She had her doubts, I could tell. But as they talked and Elvis described his mom and her job at the hospital, I could see my mother relax. Elvis was like that with adults—quiet, polite, respectful. He always said "Yes, ma'am" and "Yes, sir."

Once my mother was relaxed, I told her Elvis was a singer. Of course, I was careful not to mention anything about Sun, but I did say Elvis had made a record.

She gazed at him, impressed. "A record? Elvis, that's wonderful. What's it called?"

"'That's All Right, Mama,'" he said.

She smiled. "Isn't that sweet? A song about your mother."

On the way to the car we saw Lamont coming up the walk. He had just finished work and was wearing coveralls. I glanced around to make sure my mother wasn't watching, then stopped to say hello.

"Hey, Johnny, want to do something tonight?" he asked.

"Sorry, Lamont. I'm busy."

Lamont glanced at Elvis, who was eyeing him intently. "Something bothering you?"

Elvis said, "You're Lamont Turner. I seen you at the Grey Mule."

Lamont straightened his shoulders. "Oh, yeah?"

"How do you get your legs to move like that?"

"Who is this guy?" Lamont asked me.

"Elvis Presley. He's a singer."

Lamont looked him over. "Nice clothes. You could both come with me if you want."

"Not tonight," I said. "We have other things to do."

Lamont frowned. "Hey, man, I thought we were past this."

I knew what Lamont was like, but I didn't know if Elvis would understand.

"Can you excuse us for a second?" I asked Elvis.

Pulling Lamont aside, I said, "I met him at Sun Records. His song's going to be on the radio tonight."

"Oh, yeah," said Lamont. "I forgot you're in the music business, with big stars and all."

"Come on, Lamont. He's just a regular person."

"A regular white person."

"Don't be like that."

Lamont wiped a sleeve across his forehead. He glanced back at the Chapman house.

"You may think I'm just the hired help," he said, "but let me tell you something. People around here, they say you're the hired help too."

"What do you mean?" I asked.

"Your mother works for Chapman, same as my father and me. Only difference is, she's paying rent."

"What's wrong with that?"

He said, "I bet she gets a good deal on it."

"She keeps Mr. Chapman's books. She's been with him a long time."

"How long? Say, fifteen years?"

"Huh?"

"Nothing. Forget it. Look, you have fun with your new friend. I'll see you around."

He turned and walked off. Part of me wanted to call after him, to apologize about being busy. Another part wanted to grab him and shake him as hard as I could.

"Hey, Johnny, man, you all right?"

I looked around and saw Elvis. "Yeah, I'm fine."

"Why is he so mad?" asked Elvis.

I shook my head. "I wish I knew."

The Suzore No. 2 was a little theater downtown, just a few blocks from Elvis's house. That night they were showing a double feature: *War Paint* and *Kansas City Confidential*. I couldn't believe Elvis was sitting quietly, munching popcorn and watching people shoot each other, while his record was playing on the radio. I did notice that his hand shook as he ate his popcorn, and his knee was bouncing faster than ever.

Halfway through the second feature, a couple of shadowy figures made their way down the aisles, one on each side of the theater. They would stop at each row and look at people's faces, then move on. When they got to our row, one of them hissed, "Elvis! Elvis!"

It was Gladys Presley. The other figure was Vernon. Gladys motioned for Elvis to come, and he made his way over to the aisle, the movie images flickering across his head and shoulders. I followed along behind. Gladys grabbed his arm and marched him up the aisle and into the lobby, where Vernon met us.

Gladys turned to Elvis. Her face was red, and her eyes were wild. "That man Dewey Phillips called. He wants you down at the station as fast as you can get there."

"Did he play my record?" asked Elvis.

Vernon said, "Play it? He's wearing it out."

"He played your song seven times in a row," said Gladys. "He says the phones are ringing off the hook."

Elvis's face turned white. He swallowed hard and turned to me. "You want to come with me?"

"I sure do," I said.

Elvis kissed his mother, and we ran to the car. A few minutes later we pulled up to the Hotel Chisca and hurried inside.

Dewey did his show from the mezzanine level, just above the lobby. When we got there, he was playing Elvis's record again, breaking in every few seconds to yell "Deegaw!" and say how great it was.

Spotting Elvis, Dewey waved him over. On a table beside him was a telephone and a stack of papers.

He said, "I played your record at nine thirty, and them bird-brain phones haven't stopped ringing since. My engineer counted forty-seven calls so far. And look here." He picked up a fistful of papers. "Telegrams! Fourteen of 'em! They all want to know the same thing—who's that singer?

What's his name? Where's he from? Well, they're about to find out."

"What do you mean?" asked Elvis.

Dewey said, "Sit down. I'm gonna interview you."

Elvis turned even whiter, if that was possible. "Mr. Phillips, I don't know nothing about being interviewed."

Dewey grinned. "Just don't say anything dirty." He pulled up a chair next to him and yanked Elvis down into it. I stayed back, watching and listening.

Dewey spun another record on the turntable, and while it played he asked Elvis a few questions, like what his name was and where he had gone to high school. They talked for a few minutes about his music.

Finally Dewey said, "All right, Elvis, thank you very much."

"Aren't you going to interview me?" asked Elvis.

"I just did," said Dewey, taking off his earphones. "The mike's been open the whole time."

Elvis gulped. I noticed that he was wringing wet, like he had just stepped out of the shower. "Do you think that's enough?" he stammered.

"Hey," said Dewey, "the people got what they wanted. They know your name. They know you're from Memphis. And they know you're white, even though you may not sound like it."

"They do?" said Elvis.

"Why do you think I asked where you went to high school? Humes High is all white, and everybody knows it."

He gave Elvis a wink and slapped him on the back.

Then he put his earphones back on, grabbed the micro-phone, and cranked up the music.

Elvis may have been nervous when we walked into the studio, but by the time we left he had a grin that stretched from here to Knoxville.

We jumped into the car, and Elvis turned on the radio. Dewey was playing his song again, yelling over the music, *"You hear that, Myrtle? You can bet Mama's savings on it, 'cause Daddy-o-Dewey says it's a hit!"*

I pictured kids all over Memphis glued to their radios, listening to the song over and over again, kids bored with home and school and church, kids tired of rules, kids itch-ing for something different, something they could call their own. They couldn't tell you what they were looking for, but they knew it when they heard it. It was in that voice. It was in that loose, free, edgy, dangerous way of singing.

Elvis leaned back in the seat and closed his eyes. He stayed that way for a minute, just smiling and listening. Then he looked over at me.

"Let's go to K's," he said.

CHAPTER THIRTEEN

When we got to K's the place was jumping. People were out of their cars, milling around. The voice of Dewey Phillips blared from a dozen radios. We pulled into a parking space, got out, and leaned against the side of the car. Somebody yelled, "Hey, Elvis!"

A young man came bounding up to the car and pumped Elvis's hand. "English class at Humes High. Remember me? Man, I had no idea you were a singer!"

A couple of girls appeared behind him, giggling. One of them asked, "Are you Elvis Presley?"

Elvis's lip curled into a friendly grin. "I reckon so."

She asked, "Could I have your autograph?"

He signed her menu. As he did, Ruth Ann came by with a tray of burgers. She delivered it to a nearby car, then noticed the crowd of girls and saw me. Her smile lit up the parking lot.

"Hello, Johnny," she said.

"Hi, Ruth Ann. Have you been listening to the radio?"

"Everybody has," she said. "That record is so . . . different. But I like it."

I grinned and tilted my head toward Elvis. "That's him, you know. Elvis Presley."

She looked at him, amazed. Finally she said, "I remember you. We met last time you were here."

"I told you he was a singer," I said. "We recorded that song at Sun Records. You know, the place where I work."

Elvis smiled and held out his hand. She took it and held it, gazing into his eyes. Then she fumbled for her order pad. "I guess I should find out what you want."

She took our order and headed off. As she disappeared into the crowd, Trey Chapman pulled into a space nearby. Graydon Scarborough was with him. They got out of the car and, spotting us, wandered over. Graydon eyed Elvis, with his pink stripes and long sideburns.

"I see your friend got some new clothes," said Graydon. "Somebody should tell him the zoo's across town."

Just then a voice called out from the car radio. *"Deegaw!"*

I said, "If you're listening to Dewey Phillips, then you probably remember my friend's name. It's Elvis Presley."

Graydon stared. "*The* Elvis Presley? The guy on the radio?"

Elvis smiled shyly. Graydon turned to Trey. "They kept playing his song. Dewey interviewed him, remember?"

"Yeah, I remember," said Trey. "That was really you?"

I could tell he was impressed, though he didn't want to admit it. He took a pack of cigarettes from his shirt pocket, shook one out, and placed it between his lips. He lit up, using a silver lighter with his initials engraved on the side, and peered at Elvis.

A group of high school girls huddled off to one side. Tittering, they finally had the nerve to come closer. One of them offered Elvis a ballpoint pen.

"Can you sign my arm?" she asked.

As Elvis took the pen, Trey spotted Ruth Ann on her way to another car.

"Hey, baby," said Trey.

Ruth Ann glanced back at him and kept going. Trey stared at her.

"She's not your baby," I said.

Trey looked over at me. "What did you say?"

Suddenly my throat was dry. I swallowed. "Maybe she doesn't like you calling her that."

Trey grabbed my arm. Turning to Graydon, he said, "I'll be right back." Holding my arm in an iron grip, he hustled me off to the side.

He leaned in close. I could smell the cigarette smoke on his breath. "Ruth Ann's my girl. I'll call her whatever I want."

"You don't own her," I said.

Trey looked me up and down. "Remember that day at the house? What was the boy's name—Lamont? Remember what I told him?"

"Not really."

"You don't understand how it works around here."

He gave me a hard shove. I stumbled back, lost my balance, and fell to the pavement. Trey stepped forward and stood over me.

"Remember this picture," he said. "Me on top. You on the bottom. That's how it works."

I glanced around and saw that people were watching. Elvis had noticed too, and he came hurrying over. When Graydon tried to block his way, Elvis pushed him aside. He reached down and pulled me to my feet.

"You okay, Johnny?"

"He's fine," said Trey. "Everything's fine."

He lit up another cigarette, then turned and walked back to the car, his big shoulders swaying from side to side.

A few minutes later Ruth Ann arrived with our food. She smiled at Elvis. Trey stood off to the side with Graydon, watching her.

"Aren't you going to get my order?" asked Trey.

Ruth Ann took out her pad. "What would you like?"

"A kiss," he said.

"Hey," said Graydon, "I didn't know that was on the menu."

Trey grinned. "Easy on the mustard."

Ruth Ann gazed at him. Trey took a drag from his cigarette.

She stepped toward him and gave him a peck on the cheek. He caught her around the waist, pulled her close, and whispered something in her ear. He was smiling, but there was no humor in his eyes. Finally he let her go and turned to Graydon.

"Come on," he said. "Let's get out of here."

Climbing back into the Cadillac, he gunned the engine, and they burned rubber out of the parking lot. Ruth Ann watched him drive off. I took a step toward her, but she shook her head. Then she turned and walked away.

CHAPTER FOURTEEN

Elvis drove me home, but I didn't feel like going to bed. I kept thinking about Ruth Ann and Trey.

"You want to come inside?" I asked. "We could listen to records."

Elvis, who never seemed to get tired, agreed. When we got inside, I saw that my mother had already gone to bed. Luckily, she was a sound sleeper.

I got us a couple of RC Colas and put on "The Wild Side of Life," by Hank Thompson. Elvis sang along, never missing a word. I tried more records—Frankie Laine, Kitty Wells, Eddie Fisher, Doris Day—and the same thing happened. He knew every word to every song, whether it was blues or country or pop.

Yawning, I checked my watch. It was almost midnight.

"I think I'll turn in," I said.

"No problem," said Elvis. "I'll sleep on the couch."

"You will?"

"Hey, man, don't worry about it," he said. "I've slept in a lot worse places."

He called his mother to tell her, and I headed for bed. As I dozed off, I heard a tune that sounded like "That's All Right, Mama." Padding across the dark room, I cracked open my bedroom door and looked out.

Elvis was in the living room, softly playing his guitar and singing. When he finished, he gazed off into the distance and gave a little wave.

"Thank you very much," he murmured.

The next morning I was awakened by the sound of my mother screaming. I leaped out of bed and ran down the hall. She was standing in the bathroom doorway, curlers in her hair, cream on her face, clutching her bathrobe around her. Inside the bathroom was Elvis, gazing into the mirror and combing his hair.

"Don't worry, ma'am," he was saying. "You didn't scare me."

"Well, thank God for that," she said.

A little while later Elvis appeared at the breakfast table. As far as I knew he'd been up half the night, but that morning he looked as fresh as if he'd just walked out of Lansky's.

"That's quite an outfit," said my mother, setting out the food. "Do you hand out sunglasses with that?"

She said it with a smile, in spite of the surprise she had received earlier. There was something about Elvis that made people like him. They got mad sometimes, but not for long.

My mother took off her apron and sat down with us at

the table. "Are you excited about your new song?" she asked Elvis.

"I surely am," he said. "I want to do lots more. Not just the blues. Country, too. And gospel, like the Statesmen."

The Statesmen were one of the best-known white gospel quartets in Memphis. They performed at the all-night gospel singings held once a month at Ellis Auditorium, downtown, where Elvis was a regular.

"You like gospel quartets?" asked my mother.

"Oh yes, ma'am. I wish I could sing in one."

His features softened, and he got a faraway look in his eyes. Hearing him talk about gospel, I realized where I'd seen that look. It was in church, on my mother's face. Elvis believed in music the way she believed in God. He longed for it to lift him up and carry him off into the clouds, and he believed that one day it would.

While Elvis was dreaming, Sam was working. He needed a song to put on the other side of "That's All Right, Mama," so he scheduled another recording session on Friday. I watched while he worked with Elvis, Scotty, and Bill that day and the next, trying pop songs and more blues.

Finally, late Saturday afternoon, Bill got bored and started hamming it up, singing a bluegrass tune called "Blue Moon of Kentucky" in a high, funny-sounding voice, the way Bill Monroe did it on the radio. Elvis joined in, and Scotty played along on guitar.

In the control booth, Sam perked up. "Well, I'll be," he said. "Bill Monroe's version has three beats to the bar. They're playing it in four. Gives it kind of a bluesy feel."

He had them do it again, but it didn't feel quite right. Sam told them, "Hold on, boys, I want to try something."

He switched on a second recording machine and adjusted the dials.

"Scotty, play a few notes," he said.

Scotty did, and the notes had an odd, echoey sound, like he was in some kind of electronic cave.

I said, "What's that?"

"I call it slapback," Sam said. "What do you think?"

"I think it's strange."

Sam grinned. "Strange is good."

He leaned over to the microphone by the console, pushed a button, and said, "Okay, fellas, from the top."

They tried it again, with Bill on the bottom, Elvis floating above, and Scotty weaving in and out between them. When they finished, Sam grinned. "Well, now, that's different. That's a pop song now, nearly about."

On Monday we cut more acetates of "That's All Right, Mama," with "Blue Moon of Kentucky" on the other side. Sam and I delivered them to some of the big disc jockeys around town. By Tuesday all of them were playing it.

"Hello, Memphis!" said Bob Neal on WMPS. "I've got something special for you."

"They call him Elvis," said Dick Stuart on KWEM. "Funny name, great song."

Then there was Sleepy Eyed John on WHHM. "We'll be hearing more from Elvis Presley," he said, "I guarantee it."

Sam didn't much like Sleepy Eyed John, especially after Sleepy Eye asked if Elvis needed a manager. Sam said that Elvis already had one, then stopped at a phone booth outside, called Scotty Moore, and asked him to do it. Just like that, Elvis really did have a manager, one who wasn't likely to mess up Sam's plans.

And Sam did have plans.

CHAPTER FIFTEEN

She wore a pale green sundress, and her hair glistened.

"Hello, Johnny," said Ruth Ann.

"Hi," I said, grinning like a fool.

It was two weeks later. Ruth Ann was back with Trey, but for a moment it was like the Fourth of July. There was just Ruth Ann and me, smiling, without a care in the world.

We were at Overton Park, where Sam had scheduled Elvis to play in a big outdoor music show with Slim Whitman and some other country singers. The morning of the concert, I had seen Lamont weeding in the garden and had told him about it.

"Elvis Presley's going to play," I said. "Remember, the guy with the bright-colored clothes?"

Lamont said, "Some folks at the Grey Mule claim he's pretty good. For a white boy."

"He just sings," I said. "I don't know if it's white or black. I just like it."

"Maybe I'll drop by," said Lamont. "See what all the fuss is about."

"I'll look for you," I said.

That night I got a ride to the park with Elvis. He was wearing a new sports jacket, and Dixie Locke was with him. A pretty girl with dark hair and a nice smile, she was a sophomore at South Side High. They'd met the previous January in a Bible study class at the Assembly of God Church, and the next weekend their paths crossed again at the Rainbow Rollerdrome on Highway 78, just outside of town. Dixie had been on vacation with her family in Florida for the past two weeks, which explained why Elvis had been spending so much time with me.

We drove out east of town, past Poplar Tunes, and pretty soon Overton Park rose up in front of us. It was a big place, ten blocks square and surrounded by beautiful homes. There was a large shaded area with rows of benches that sloped down to a stage and bandshell. It held a couple thousand people, and that night the place was jammed. They had come out early, maybe because of the heat, and had brought their picnic baskets with them.

Dixie and I dropped Elvis off backstage and went around front, where she spotted some of her church friends and went to sit with them. I headed up the aisle to the top for a better view. On the way I saw Vernon and Gladys Presley, with Elvis's grandmother and a whole row of people who looked like Vernon. A little farther up I saw Ruth Ann. I wanted to reach out and touch her but couldn't bring myself to do it.

"Did you come with Elvis?" she asked. "I hear he's going to sing."

I nodded. "I just dropped him off backstage. He's pretty nervous, but I think I calmed him down."

"I can't believe you actually know him," she said.

A hand appeared on her shoulder. I looked up and saw Trey Chapman. Graydon Scarborough was with him.

"What's going on here?" said Trey.

Ruth Ann looked up nervously. "We were just talking about Elvis."

"Hey, Trey," said Graydon, "what's pink and black and white all over?"

"A zebra with a sunburn?"

Graydon grinned. "No, man. Elvis Presley."

Ignoring him, Ruth Ann gazed at me, as if she wanted to say something. Like, *I'm sorry. I miss you. Don't worry about him.* Then again, maybe it was my imagination.

Trey said, "Ruth Ann's sitting in the front row, with us. Where are you?"

"I thought I'd watch from the top."

"You'll need binoculars if you want to see Elvis," said Trey. He put his arm around Ruth Ann. "Or anybody else." Then he said, "Come on. I see some friends."

I nodded to Ruth Ann. "Enjoy the concert."

"You too," she said.

I watched her leave, then continued up the aisle. When I reached the top, I saw another familiar face. Lamont was standing behind the back row. Seeing him fidget uncomfortably, I asked, "Are you all right?"

"I don't like this crowd," he said.

I looked out at the people, surprised. "They seem okay to me."

"Course they do. You're white."

I looked at the crowd again. Lamont was the only Negro there. Standing with him, it was as if I'd put on a pair of glasses that allowed me to see the world in a different way. Suddenly the place didn't seem quite so friendly. I wondered what it must be like to wear those glasses all the time.

A few minutes later the lights went down, and Bob Neal stepped to the microphone. I had never seen him, but I recognized his voice from the radio.

"Hello, Memphis!" he said. "We've got a great show for you tonight. We've got Billy Walker, with his debut record 'Thank You for Calling.'"

There was scattered applause.

"We've got Slim Whitman . . . well, I reckon you know Slim."

The crowd let out a big cheer.

"And we've got a special treat for you tonight. You've heard his records on the radio. Now you can hear him in person—Memphis's own Elvis Presley!"

There were some cheers from down in front, where Dixie's group was sitting. Next to me, somebody laughed. "Elvis who? What kind of name is that?"

Billy Walker came out first, but I barely heard him. I remembered how jumpy Elvis had been backstage, and I wondered how he would do in front of all those people. What if they didn't clap? What if he was too scared to sing?

When Billy Walker finished, Bob Neal did his best to get the crowd excited about Elvis, but they seemed more interested in their fried chicken and barbecue. Then the lights went down again and Elvis, Scotty, and Bill came out. They looked awfully small on that big stage.

Elvis adjusted the microphone, took a deep breath, and played the opening chords of "That's All Right, Mama." The crowd perked up. A few people seemed to know the song from hearing it on the radio. When Elvis started to sing, I turned to Lamont.

"What do you think?" I asked.

"He's doing a blues song, but it isn't the blues," said Lamont. "I don't know what it is."

Just then the crowd let out a roar. I looked down at the stage and saw that something odd was happening. Elvis wasn't standing flat-footed, the way he usually did. He was up on the balls of his feet, and his legs were jiggling and shaking. The crowd loved it. They whooped and hollered, and the more they hollered, the more Elvis shook. After the verse, he backed off from the mike, and his knees started pumping like pistons, up and down, side to side, back and forth. Something about it was familiar, but I couldn't think what. Then I glanced sideways, and I knew.

Lamont was staring at the stage, his face twisted in anger. Suddenly I was back at the Grey Mule, standing in the doorway, watching Lamont play. I had studied his hands and face, but it was his legs that fascinated me. They whipped and gyrated, knees bumping together and circling out again.

"Those are my moves," said Lamont. "He stole my moves."

I said, "Elvis is always jiggling around like that. Maybe he's just nervous."

Lamont said, "He stole Arthur Crudup's music, and now he stole my moves."

Lamont took a step forward. For a minute I thought he was going to charge the stage, but he caught himself and looked around. He stood there, clenching and unclenching his fists. Then he turned and headed off, away from the crowd.

Meanwhile, Elvis finished his first number and swung into "Blue Moon of Kentucky." By that time the people had forgotten their fried chicken and were on their feet, dancing and jumping around. Judging from the looks of the crowd I was pretty sure most of them had never heard Elvis's record, but it didn't seem to matter. The music had grabbed them, and Elvis's wild motions had jolted them into action as surely as if they'd been struck by lightning. Every time Elvis shook his leg they let out another yell, and he'd shake it again. He might have seemed shy at first, but he was turning out to be a quick learner.

The song stopped, but the crowd didn't. They wanted more. Elvis and the others had walked off the stage, and the people stamped their feet and chanted until he came back, a big grin on his face. He sang "Blue Moon of Kentucky" as an encore. Bill beat on the bass like it was a drum, and Elvis's motions were even wilder.

After the show I hurried backstage, where I found Scotty, Bill, and Elvis, who had his arm around Dixie. They were talking to Doug Poindexter and the other Starlite Wranglers. The Wranglers didn't seem too happy.

They hadn't seen much of Scotty or Bill since Elvis came along.

I said to Elvis, "Man, the crowd loved that thing you did with your leg. What was it?"

"I'm not sure," he said. "I didn't even know I was doing anything till the crowd hollered. I was scared stiff."

Scotty said, "Whatever it was, keep doing it."

Just then a large, sad-faced man came through the crowd. I recognized him from my trips to radio stations with Sam, when we dropped off the acetates. The man took out his wallet and handed Elvis a business card.

"Sleepy Eyed John, over at WHHM," he said. "I also book the Eagle's Nest, out at Clearpool."

Clearpool was a swimming complex east of town. I'd been there a few times with my mother, and I'd heard there was a club on the second floor, over the changing rooms, where they held dances on weekends.

"I'd love to get you out there," said Sleepy Eye. "My band plays on Saturday nights, and we need somebody to come on when we take a break. What do you say?"

Scotty stepped forward. "He doesn't say anything without me. I'm his manager."

Doug Poindexter grabbed hold of Scotty's arm. "What about the Starlite Wranglers?" he said. "Tell him about us."

Scotty shook his head. "Can't do it. They don't want hillbilly music."

Doug glanced at Elvis, then back at Scotty. "Okay, here's the deal. Either it's him or us. It's time to choose."

Scotty turned to Bill. A look passed between them, and Scotty nodded. He turned back to the Wranglers.

"Sorry, boys," he said.

Doug took a step back, not quite believing it. Then he scowled and stomped off, with his friends behind him.

Scotty finished up with Sleepy Eyed John. A few minutes later, Elvis was booked into the Eagle's Nest, starting the following week. With the Wranglers out of the picture, I guess Scotty decided he and Bill needed a new name, so he told Sleepy Eye that Elvis would be backed up by the Blue Moon Boys.

After Sleepy Eye left, Scotty grinned and slapped Elvis on the back. "Well, I'd say tonight was a big success. We might actually have to learn more than two songs."

Elvis gave him that shy smile. It was hard to believe he was the same person who had been shaking his legs and jumping around the stage.

I remembered Lamont's look of helpless rage as he had watched. I thought of the anger in his eyes, and in the eyes of the Starlite Wranglers backstage. The concert had gone well, but for a big success it sure had made a lot of people mad.

CHAPTER SIXTEEN

I didn't sleep well that night. I saw Elvis on the ceiling, shaking his legs. Lamont watched him, furious, then stomped off. I wondered where Lamont had gone and if he was all right.

When I woke up Saturday morning, there was a note from my mother saying she had gone shopping. I took a shower and got some cereal, all the while thinking about Lamont. I wanted to go see him but realized that I didn't know where he lived. I couldn't look up his number because I didn't know his mother's name, so instead I called Irene, the Chapmans' maid. She gave me Lamont's address, on Wellington, near Vance Avenue in town.

I took the bus to Vance Avenue, and as I approached town the area started looking familiar. At the corner of Wellington there was a sign: WILLIAM H. FOOTE HOMES.

Suddenly it all made sense. That night when we had gone driving, Lamont had naturally headed for the area he knew best—Foote Homes, his home. Maybe he had been embarrassed to tell me he lived in a housing project, especially knowing the neighborhood where I lived. Maybe he had planned to tell me but had been distracted by the burning cross. In any case, I had never found out where he lived or taken the trouble to learn, even though I thought I was his friend.

I got off at Fourth Street and walked back to Wellington. There were Negroes all around, sitting on the porch, working in the yard. Some of them stared. I pretended not to notice. I found Lamont's address. It was a small brick apartment with potted flowers on the porch.

I knocked, but there was no answer. I knocked again and finally the door opened. Lamont stood there with a bottle in his hand.

"Well, well, well," he said. "It's Johnny Ross."

I could smell the liquor on his breath. I said, "Maybe I should leave. I can come back."

He spread out his arms. "What do you think of this place? 'Nice homes for Negroes.' Almost as nice as yours, huh?"

"It's fine," I said. "You know, that night when we came here? You could have told me. It would have been all right."

He gave a flick of his hand. "Who cares? You're here now. Come on in."

I hesitated, then stepped inside. It was a modest but neatly kept place. Lamont studied me as I looked around.

He said, "You got to admit, it's clean. That's what happens when your mother's a maid."

"Where is she?" I asked.

"She works on Saturday. 'Dirt doesn't take a day off.' That's what she says. Sometimes she even goes in on Sunday after church if the people are having a big dinner."

He took a swig from the bottle. "Hey, man, you want something to drink?"

"That's okay," I said.

"How about a Coca-Cola?"

I nodded. He went to the kitchen and came back holding my drink. As he handed it to me, he lifted his bottle. "You want some of this in it?"

"No, thanks," I said.

He settled heavily onto the sofa. I sat down in a chair across from him.

"You missed some good music last night," I said. "The crowd really liked it."

"If they want to see something, they should go down to Beale Street, like Elvis Presley did. Isn't that right?"

"He loves the blues," I said.

Lamont scowled. "He took a good, stiff bourbon and changed it into a milk shake. The blues should burn going down. It should make you flinch. He made it sweet. That's not the blues."

"Maybe it's something new," I said.

"Ain't nothing new," said Lamont.

He heaved himself to his feet and walked across the room, where he put on a record. A scratchy, high-pitched voice came from the speaker: *"I'm gonna leave you baby, I'm gonna leave you all alone."*

The singer backed up his words with guitar playing like

I'd never heard before. The notes stretched and glided, then circled around and back.

"Who is that?" I asked.

"Muddy Waters. I used to hear him play in Chicago."

"How does he do it?"

"It's called the slide. He rolls a bottleneck on the strings so the notes bend up and down."

"I don't mean the slide. I mean the music."

Lamont said, "The blues? It's hard. Nothing harder. You gotta work till the sound fades away and all that's left is the feelings. You feeling bad today? You feeling good? Tell it in the music. You angry? You so mad you want to grab somebody and rip him in two? Then play it. Sing it."

I thought about the anger on Lamont's face as he had watched Elvis Presley the night before.

"You really think Elvis stole from you?" I asked.

"Not just me. What about Arthur Crudup? You think he'll ever see a dime of royalties?"

"Royalties?" I said. "What's that?"

Lamont laughed bitterly. "That's what the producers say. All of them, including Sam Phillips. Listen, man, you know what Arthur Crudup's doing right now? He's sitting on a tractor someplace, plowing a field. You know what he'll be doing if his song's a hit?"

"What?"

"Sitting on a tractor, plowing a field. They won't pay him nothing." He looked at me and sighed. "Every time they sell a record, the songwriter's supposed to get paid. That's royalties. Only it don't work that way if you're Negro. You make a few dollars when they cut the record, and that's the last you see. Especially blues singers. Most of them come straight out of the fields. How are they supposed to know about royalties? Man, they're just happy to get paid."

I said, "It's a good song. I like the way Elvis sings it."

Lamont shook his head. "No white boy can sing the blues. That's a fact."

"Some people think he sounds black," I said.

He studied my face for a minute, as if he were looking for something. "Come on, Johnny, you're smarter than that."

I shrugged. "Sam Phillips says it's true."

"You ask Sam Phillips when he's going to pay Arthur Crudup. Then we'll see what he says."

Shaking his head, Lamont turned back to the record player. When the music ended, he took a drink from his bottle.

"So, here we are," he said. "A nice white boy and a poor, sad Nee-gro."

"Come on, Lamont. What are you doing?"

"What does it look like?"

I nodded toward the bottle. "Why don't you put that away?"

"This? No, no, this is my friend." He held it up to the light. "It won't hurt me. It won't cheat me. It won't take what's rightfully mine."

I said, "Last night at the park, you sure left in a hurry."

"It was either that or break the rule," he said.

"Rule?"

"The rule says a Negro can't get mad at white people. He can smile. He can dance. He can play music. He can cook their food and wash their dishes and clean up their trash. But he can't get mad. No, sir, that wouldn't be right."

Lamont took another drink from the bottle and looked past me, at things I'd never seen or imagined.

"Do you know about the bombing?" he asked.

"What bombing?"

"It happened a year ago. A Negro family bought a house in a white neighborhood, and the neighbors didn't like it."

"In Memphis?" I asked.

He nodded. "On Olive Street. Somebody sneaked up in the middle of the night and put a bomb on the porch. Nobody was hurt, but the house was damaged. Funny thing is, the police never caught the bomber. They had better things to do."

"I never heard about any of it," I said.

"I did. It was my aunt and uncle. Remember when I told you my mother had relatives in Memphis, and they got her a job? That's who it was—Uncle Wren and Aunt Florence. Some redneck bombs their house, and a few months later they ask their sister to move on down. Heat's on, pot's boiling. Come on in, the water's fine. Welcome to Foote Homes. Just watch out for the burning cross."

I said, "When you talk about Memphis, it sounds like a different place from where I live."

"You're smart, Johnny. You think about that. Then do yourself a favor, huh? Get out of Memphis. Go to Chicago. Go to New York. First chance you get, you leave and don't look back."

CHAPTER SEVENTEEN

Trey wanted me to forget about Ruth Ann, but I couldn't. I was thinking about her at work on Monday, when Sam showed up and announced he was hitting the road. He would travel across the South, calling on distributors, disc jockeys, jukebox operators, and record store owners, telling them about Elvis, playing the record and selling it. He asked me to help out Marion while he was gone.

"Look, here's what I'm thinking," he said. "I'll pay you for the next couple of weeks. We'll see how it goes. How does that sound?"

There had been a time, not long before, when having Sam offer me a job would have meant the world to me. Now it didn't seem as important. The truth was that I just liked being there. I slept in the cottage on Belvedere Boulevard, but in some way I didn't understand, Sun Records had become my home.

Even so, I had to smile. "Thanks, Mr. Phillips. You won't regret it."

As I worked that week, I kept thinking about Ruth Ann. I wondered what it would be like to see her again.

I got my chance sooner than I expected.

With the Starlite Wranglers out of the picture, Scotty and Bill turned their full attention to Elvis. In the mornings Scotty worked for his brother at University Park Cleaners on the east side of town, and later in the day his brother would let them use an upstairs room to practice in. The room had a Coke machine and a beat-up sofa, and pretty soon Scotty, Bill, and Elvis had made it their own.

They would meet there in the afternoons, and Bill or Scotty would usually bring a bag of burgers and fries from the Dairy Dip. Elvis never brought the food, but he was more than happy to eat it. Then, when he was finished with his, he would reach over and snag fries from the others. If somebody asked him to chip in to pay for the food, he would just shrug and pull out an empty wallet. It was empty so often, I wondered why he carried it at all. It reminded me of how, when I visited his house, he had let someone else clean up after him. Elvis wanted to be a star, but in a way he had been treated like one his whole life.

I dropped by the practices whenever I could. While Elvis or Scotty would run the band through some new numbers, I would sit on the sofa with Dixie, leaning forward, hanging on every note.

After practice, Scotty and Bill's wives, Bobbie and Evelyn, would come by. Together with Elvis and Dixie, the couples would gather around an old wooden sorting table and eat spaghetti that Evelyn had brought, along with a bottle of cheap Italian wine. I would sit with them, watching, eating but not really a part of the group. I found myself imagining Ruth Ann at the table, sitting beside me, laughing and talking with the others.

It was hard to picture Ruth Ann without thinking of Trey. I remembered the way he had shoved me. He had shoved Lamont, too. But Lamont didn't just lie there. He had jumped back up, ready to fight. As I thought about it, anger began to well up inside me. I could spend my life on the ground, or I could get to my feet and do something.

I called Ruth Ann on Wednesday. My voice was quivering and my throat was dry, but she didn't seem to notice. I told her about the rehearsals and asked if she would like to come to one. I had figured that making the call was the important thing, and that Ruth Ann would turn me down. To my surprise, she said yes.

At Sun Records later that day, Marion called me into the front room. She reached into the desk drawer and pulled out a check.

"That's for your work this week," she said. "Don't spend it all in one place."

I immediately thought of Elvis. When he got his first check from Sam, he had headed straight for Lansky's. I wasn't ready to do that, but I did want to look nice. I cashed the check and went down the street to a little clothing store, where I bought some khakis and a short-sleeved shirt.

When I got home, I tried on the clothes and gazed at

myself in the mirror. Remembering Elvis, I rolled up the sleeves and slicked back my hair. Then I put a rubber band around the rest of the money, hid it in a dresser drawer, and got ready to see Ruth Ann.

Elvis came by to pick me up in the Lincoln coupe, with Dixie at his side. He gave me a hard time about my clothes, saying I would look better in pink and black, but when I went to Ruth Ann's door she said I looked nice. I walked her to the car, feeling like a king.

I should have known it wouldn't be easy. When we entered the rehearsal room, Bill called out, "Scotty, better tell your brother. Johnny's been stealing clothes from the dry cleaners."

"Now, Bill," said Evelyn, "don't give him a hard time. Who's your friend, Johnny?"

"This is Ruth Ann Morris," I said proudly.

"Pleased to meet you," said Ruth Ann, offering her hand. She was radiant in a yellow dress. There was something about Ruth Ann that allowed her to fit into any setting—rich or not-so-rich, fancy or plain, school or church or beat-up rehearsal room.

We dug into the spaghetti. Ruth Ann, Dixie, and I sipped RC Colas, while the others drank wine. It seemed to relax Elvis, and he started talking. As usual, the topic was himself—in this case, what would happen when he made it big. The odd thing was, he didn't seem to be boasting. He spoke quietly, in a matter-of-fact way.

"The first thing I'll do," he said, "is buy my mother a house."

"You going to let your father stay there?" asked Bill.

"Oh, yeah," said Elvis, not getting the joke. "Probably my grandmother, too."

"That's sweet," said Bobbie.

"The second thing," he said, "is to get me a brand-new Cadillac convertible. Pink, maybe. Or gold. I'll let you all ride in it if you're good."

Grinning that funny sideways grin of his, he winked at Evelyn. She rolled her eyes.

"Of course," he said casually, "my real goal isn't records at all."

"What is it?" asked Ruth Ann.

"Movies. Like Cary Grant. Like Glen Ford and Rory Calhoun. You know."

"Hey, man," said Scotty, "you just cut your first record. Maybe you didn't notice, but we're eating spaghetti, not caviar. And this isn't Hollywood. It's Memphis, Tennessee."

"Just watch," said Elvis. "You'll see."

Ruth Ann glanced over at me, not sure what to think.

I said, "He's different, isn't he?"

Dixie moved closer to Elvis and put her hand on his.

"He's crazy," said Scotty. "Lucky for us, he can sing."

He proved it over the next couple of hours. The group ran through a dozen or more songs—country, pop, gospel, and the blues. After rehearsing, they gathered around the piano to sing a few hymns, and the rest of us joined in. Elvis, as always, knew the words to every one.

In the middle of "Just as I Am," there was a new voice. I looked around and saw Wynette Pugh. Her mother worked at the cleaners, and little Wynette liked to come upstairs and watch the band rehearse. We had never paid much attention to her, but now we did. She may have been only twelve, but her voice turned out to be huge and at least thirty-five.

When the hymn was over, Bill joked, "Hey, Wynette, want to sing with the band?"

She said yes. Next thing we knew, Bill and Scotty were laying down a beat, and Wynette was doing her version of "How High the Moon," by Les Paul and Mary Ford. Elvis and Dixie started to dance, and Ruth Ann looked over at me.

"What do you think, Johnny?" she said.

Gulping, I followed her to an empty space on the floor. The song was fast, so we did the jitterbug, or at least Ruth Ann did. I followed along as well as I could. Then Wynette moved to a ballad, "I Cried," by Patti Page. While I tried to figure out what to do, Ruth Ann slid into my arms as easily as you'd slip into a comfortable sweater. She was soft but felt strong and sure. Her hair smelled like roses. Up close, I saw green flecks in her eyes.

I wondered what Trey would do if he saw us. I must have pulled back for a second, because Ruth Ann whispered, "What's wrong, Johnny?"

I moved closer again. "Nothing," I murmured. "Nothing at all."

Several minutes or maybe it was hours later, the song ended. Wynette, her voice as big as a house, started another ballad.

"Hey, Johnny," said Elvis, "let's switch."

Before I knew what had happened, I was dancing with

Dixie, and Elvis was holding Ruth Ann. Dixie felt different—taller, leaner, not nearly as soft. It didn't help that she kept craning her neck to watch Elvis and Ruth Ann. I had to admit, so did I. We moved around the dance floor, swiveling our heads like a couple of storks.

Elvis was smiling at Ruth Ann. His lips were moving, but I couldn't make out what he was saying. His body moved with hers. I was struck by how long his arms were, wrapped all the way around her.

For Ruth Ann's part, she seemed nervous at first, holding herself stiffly, leaving space in between. Then she giggled at something Elvis said and moved in closer. As she did, Dixie and I moved apart, until we were dancing at arm's length, barely in the same county.

"What's he doing?" hissed Dixie.

I didn't reply. I knew that if I opened my mouth I'd start yelling. I wasn't sure what I'd do after that.

Wynette swung into the last verse, and Elvis gathered Ruth Ann closer. When she put her head on his shoulder, something inside me cracked.

"Get away from her!" I shouted.

The music halted. So did Elvis and Ruth Ann.

I sputtered, "What do you think you're doing?"

Elvis shrugged. "Dancing."

I looked around. Everybody was staring.

Bobbie smiled as she studied me. "Well, what do you know. I believe he's jealous."

I walked up to Elvis, my hands shaking. "I said, get away."

He looked me over. The place was silent. Then he said, "Sure, man. No problem."

He stepped back from Ruth Ann, but she continued to gaze at him. As I wondered what to do next, Evelyn came up behind me and took my arm. She walked me over to a corner.

"Get over it, baby. That's just Elvis being Elvis. It's nothing personal."

It seemed personal to me. I watched as he sauntered across the room to a mirror, took out his comb, and started fooling with his hair.

I had thought Elvis was my friend, but sometimes it seemed that I hardly knew him. I said so to Evelyn, and she smiled.

"See that mirror?" she said. "That's Elvis. People find whatever they want to in him. None of it's real. It's just a reflection."

I watched Elvis smooth his hair and flash himself a grin. To Dixie he was a dreamboat. To Sam he was a meal ticket. To my mother he was a nice young man. To Lamont he was a thief. To the people at Overton Park he was pure energy, raw and uncut. I tried to imagine what was behind that smile of his. I wondered if I would ever find out.

CHAPTER EIGHTEEN

When I got home it was after ten o'clock. The lights were on, which wasn't unusual. My mother was still awake, which was. She was sitting on the sofa when I came through the front door.

"How was the rehearsal?" she asked.

"Fine."

I had told her about the sessions at the dry cleaners, including the spaghetti suppers. I hadn't mentioned anything about Ruth Ann. It seemed private, along with a growing list of things in my life that I'd been keeping to myself.

"Johnny, sit down," she said.

I sat in a chair opposite her, feeling uncomfortable. She reached behind her and pulled out a roll of bills held together by a rubber band.

"Hey, that's mine," I said.

"I found it in your room."

"You went into my dresser. You shouldn't have done that. It's private."

She crossed her arms. "Where did you get it?"

I didn't answer.

"Where, Johnny? I need to know."

For a minute I considered telling her about my job at Sun Records. But I was afraid that if I did, she might make me quit.

"It doesn't matter," I said.

"I talked to Will," she said. "He told me you've been spending time with Lamont, after I specifically told you not to. Why, Johnny?"

"I like him," I said.

"Did you steal this money?"

"What?"

"Did you steal it? What have you and Lamont been doing?"

I stared at her. "Is that what you think? That he's some kind of criminal?"

"Where did you get the money?"

I thought about the time Lamont had told me he stole his car. It had been a test, and I had wondered why he did it. Now I knew. Some people really believed it. They thought that, like the blues, like the clothing at Lansky's, like fried chicken and watermelons, stealing was something that came with being a Negro. And it seemed that my mother was one of those people.

"I didn't steal it," I said. "Neither did Lamont. He's my friend."

"No, he's not!"

"He plays the blues. He's good."

She said, "The blues! That's Negro music."

"So what? What does that even mean?"

"I wish it didn't mean anything," she said. "I wish we lived in a better world. But we don't. So there are certain things we do. And don't do."

"Not me."

"Will said he told you the same thing. Stay away from Lamont. And you deliberately ignored him."

I got up and walked to the window. It was dark outside.

I said, "I'm tired of people telling me what to do."

"Oh, please. You come and go as you want. You run around at night. Half the time I don't even know where you are. The one thing I asked was that you stay away from Lamont."

"What's wrong with Lamont?" I said. "He's a person. He has a father. He has relatives. I've seen pictures of them."

"Pictures? Where?"

"At Will's house."

"His *house*?"

"I went there a few weeks ago."

She got to her feet and paced across the room, shaking her head. "Lord, what have I done?"

"It's nice," I said. "It's the kind of place I'd like to live in someday."

She stopped in front of me and put her face close to mine. "Have I raised you in a bubble? Don't you see? This is Memphis. Color matters. I'm white. You're white. Lamont is black. We don't mix."

I said, "I'll see him if I want to."

"No, you won't. I forbid it."

"You can't tell me what to do," I said.

She moved up close to me. "Yes, I can."

Her gaze bore into me like a drill. I stepped back. Stumbling, I crossed to my room, pulled the door shut, and locked it.

I heard footsteps and the rattle of the doorknob.

"Johnny, let me in. Johnny?"

There was a knock on the door. It got louder.

"Johnny!"

Finally it turned into pounding.

"Johnny!"

I switched on the radio and tuned it to WHBQ. There was a blues record playing. It sounded like Muddy Waters.

The pounding got louder.

"Johnny!" called my mother.

"Deegaw!" said Dewey Phillips.

I stayed in my room the next morning. My mother knocked again. Her voice was muffled, like she'd been crying. I didn't answer. A little while later she left for work.

I got dressed and made myself a bowl of cereal. I thought about my mother looking through my dresser, pulling out my things, accusing me of stealing. I thought of her talking to Will, and suddenly I needed to see him.

I found Will in his room off the garage, where he kept his tools and chauffeur's clothing. When he answered the door, he was just putting on a jacket and straightening his tie.

Looking nervously across the yard, he said, "You should leave. Mr. Chapman will be here in a minute."

"You spoke to my mother," I said. "You told her I was with Lamont."

He started to close the door. "Let's talk about this later."

I blocked the door with my foot and pushed past him into the room. Looking around, I realized I'd never been inside. There was a desk, with papers stacked neatly on top, and a telephone. Gardening tools hung on the walls, grouped by size and function. There was an African rug on the floor like the one at his house. A corner of the room had been converted to a closet, and in it, neatly pressed, were gardening clothes and chauffeur's suits. Off to one side was a bathroom with a shower.

Will's hand closed around my arm like a vise. "You have to leave."

"I want to talk," I said.

Will glanced over my shoulder and stopped in his tracks. I turned to see what he was looking at. Arthur Chapman was standing in the doorway. He stared at Will, then at me.

I remembered a time when I was ten years old. I had been playing in the yard one Saturday. The wind had been blowing all afternoon, and suddenly it stopped. My mother came running out of the house, calling my name. She grabbed me and pulled me inside. As the screen door slammed shut behind us, I glanced back and got one last look at the sky. It wasn't blue. It wasn't gray or black. It was a color I'd never seen before, a kind of vivid pink, the color of blood. We ran into the hallway. A minute later, the tornado hit. The house survived and so did we, but I've never forgotten the color of that sky.

It was the color of Mr. Chapman's face as he stared at us. A terrible calm settled over him. He said, "Johnny, I think you'd better go home. Mr. Turner, I'll see you in my office in five minutes."

He turned and walked back to the house, his shoulders stiff and straight.

Will watched him leave. His face had a haunted look, like some ghost from the past was bearing down on him.

"What happened?" I asked.

"Go," he said. "Get out of here."

I felt angry and guilty and bewildered all at the same time. I wanted to say something but had no idea what.

I walked to the door. Will gazed at me sadly. We were just a few feet apart, but it seemed like miles.

"I don't understand," I said.

"Neither do I," said Will. And he closed the door.

At supper that night my mother seemed quiet. Finally she said, "I missed you today."

"Huh?"

"It was Thursday. Lunch at the Peabody."

"Oh, I'm sorry. I forgot."

She said, "I didn't really expect you to come. You know, after last night."

I nodded.

"After lunch, Mr. Chapman called me into his office."

I looked up at her. She had been angry the night before,

but this time I saw something different in her eyes. It was fear.

"Was it about Will?" I asked.

"It seems that you were in the garage with him."

"So?"

"We don't do that," she said.

I thought of all the times my mother had told me to stay away from Will. She'd been doing it my whole life. Recently she'd added Lamont. I didn't understand it. What was the harm in talking to someone? Folks did it, even in Memphis, including some of the worst bigots in town— white people and Negroes, passing in the street, saying hello, visiting. It was okay for them, but not for me. Why?

I didn't know the answer, but after what had happened that morning I knew who was behind it. It wasn't my mother. It wasn't Will. It was Arthur Chapman.

Why had he been so upset to see me in the garage? What did he know that I didn't? Why did he have such a hold over Will and my mother? Was it just their jobs, or was there more?

I said, "Do you think Will's in trouble?"

"Mr. Chapman was pretty upset."

"Will won't lose his job, will he?"

"No," she said. "But I think he was probably reminded about the rules."

"What rules? What did he do wrong? I don't understand."

"It's complicated."

"You know, it was my fault, not his. At the garage today, he told me not to come in. He didn't even want me to be there."

She studied my face, as if looking for something. "Johnny, baby, listen to me. Just do as I say. Don't go to Will's house. Don't talk to him. Stay away from him. He's a good man, but he's trouble."

I gazed back at her. "I didn't think we were like that."

"The world is like that," she said.

CHAPTER NINETEEN

Lamont pulled up to the curb in his blue Ford, one hand on the wheel and the other clutching a whiskey bottle. Beside him, a newspaper was open to a small article on the back page: CROSS BURNERS RELEASED.

It was Saturday night, and Elvis was scheduled to play for the first time at the Eagle's Nest. Bill had gone over early to set up. Elvis had gone early too, since Dixie had some family obligations and couldn't be there.

I had been waiting at the curb for Scotty to pick me up when Lamont came by. I glanced back toward our house, where my mother had dozed off a few minutes earlier. I hoped she was still sleeping.

Lamont leaned across and opened the passenger door. "Come on," he said. "Let's go to Beale Street." I could smell the alcohol on his breath.

I said, "Man, are you crazy? Didn't you hear what happened?"

"You mean Chapman?" he said. "Sure. My father told me. What else is new?"

I looked around anxiously. "I can't talk to you. I have other plans."

"Is it that singer? Elvis?"

I nodded. "He's playing at the Eagle's Nest, out on Highway 78."

Lamont pushed the newspaper toward me. "I thought you might like to see this," he said. "The judge let 'em go. Said it was a 'harmless prank'."

Reading the article, I thought back to that night. I remembered the faces of the people who lived in Foote Homes. They didn't think it was a prank.

Lamont said, "If we were in Chicago those boys would be in jail. Man, I'm sick of this place. White people pushing you around. KKK burning crosses. The police are in on it, and Negroes are scared to do anything. Like my father with Chapman."

He took a long pull from the bottle.

I said, "I'm sorry, Lamont. I'd like to go to Beale Street. I just can't."

"Yeah," he mumbled. "Okay."

He closed the door, and the Ford rumbled off down the street. A few minutes later Scotty arrived, and we drove off to Clearpool. When we got there, people were lined up out the door, many of them teenagers. Scotty spotted some friends and stopped to talk. I headed for the back entrance, looking for Elvis.

The Eagle's Nest wasn't anything fancy—just a big room on the second floor over the swimming pool lockers, with a stage on one side and an area behind it where the musicians hung out between sets. The backstage area was crowded, and I bumped into someone who was coming out. I was surprised to see that it was Ruth Ann. She seemed surprised too.

"What are you doing here?" she asked.

"Looking for Elvis," I said. "Where's Trey?"

"He's not here," she said.

My heart started to race. I blurted, "Me and Elvis and the guys, we'll probably go out for a milk shake afterward. Want to come?"

"Oh, Johnny, I'm sorry. I can't." She looked around. "I need to go." As she brushed by, I got a whiff of her perfume, mixed with smoke from the crowd. For a moment I wondered why she was there, but soon I was caught up again in the excitement of the crowd and the music.

There was a little room backstage, and when I approached, Elvis came out, combing his hair.

He said, "Hey, Johnny, how's it going?"

Bill was nearby, tuning up. "Elvis, did you see that crowd?"

"I sure did," said Elvis. "They kept staring at me."

"I can't imagine why," said Bill.

Elvis was wearing another Lansky Brothers outfit, this one featuring a bolero jacket, a yellow striped shirt, tailored pants, and two-toned shoes. He grinned shyly. It occurred to me that Elvis's shy grin was as much a part of his outfit as the flashy clothes and slicked-back hair.

While Elvis got out his guitar, I went around the front of the stage to watch the show. The place was jammed.

Sleepy Eyed John and his band were playing, but, judging by the way people talked over the music, he wasn't the one they had come to see. There were no empty seats, so I moved to the back of the room and stood against the wall.

The band finished their set, and Sleepy Eye stepped up to the microphone.

"All right, now," he said, "I know who you've been waiting for."

Somebody called out, "Elvis!" The crowd laughed and applauded.

Sleepy Eye smiled. "You've heard him on the radio. Now you'll hear him at the Eagle's Nest. Ladies and gentlemen, Elvis Presley and the Blue Moon Boys!"

Elvis, Scotty, and Bill came bouncing out onto the stage. The crowd cheered, craning their necks to get a better view. Then Elvis started to sing "That's All Right, Mama," and the place went crazy. Memphis had never seen anything quite like Elvis Presley. They had never heard anything like him either. Maybe nobody had.

Elvis was on the balls of his feet again, hips swiveling, legs gyrating even more wildly than at Overton Park. The room was alive, pulsing like Scotty's guitar, thumping like Bill's big bass.

There was a disturbance off to our left. I tried to see what was going on but couldn't. Heads turned, and people craned their necks. I heard a voice, rough and ragged.

"Hey, you! Elvis Presley!"

Off to my left, in an ocean of white, a dark face appeared. I froze. It was Lamont.

"Stop playing, man!" he shouted. "You can't do that!"

Lamont gestured wildly at Elvis, his face contorted. I could tell he'd had more to drink.

"Ain't your song," he said. "Ain't your music. You stole it!"

Onstage, Elvis and the others kept playing. Scotty and Bill saw what was happening, but I'm not sure Elvis even noticed.

Lamont lurched toward the stage. Hands reached out and stopped him. I moved forward, hoping to help.

Then someone yelled, "What's that nigger doing here?"

"Get him out," said someone else. "Shut him up."

I hesitated. The crowd closed in around him. Lamont looked up and saw me.

"Johnny!" he cried.

I didn't move. I didn't speak. I watched as the bouncer, a burly man with a crew cut, waded in.

"Johnny, it's me!" said Lamont.

Suddenly the room seemed hot and crowded. Faces swirled in front of me. A drop of sweat dripped down my lip. It tasted salty and bitter.

A girl came up beside me. "Do you know him?"

Lamont gazed at me, his eyes pleading.

I shook my head. "No, I don't."

The bouncer grabbed Lamont and dragged him off.

CHAPTER TWENTY

I didn't hear much of the music after that. I kept thinking about Lamont. I remembered the way he had looked at me, and I wondered what had happened after they took him away. After a few more songs I slipped out the back. The bouncer was standing outside, next to the door.

"Excuse me," I said, "could you tell me what happened to the guy you brought outside?"

"The nigger?" he said.

I didn't answer. I didn't want to say yes to that word.

He repeated, "The nigger? Is that who you mean?"

Who was I kidding? I thought I didn't like the word, but I had stood there and watched while they dragged Lamont off. I was a part of it, just like everybody else in the room.

"Yes," I said.

"He was lucky," said the man. "I told him to go home and sleep it off."

When I went back inside, Elvis was just finishing up. The crowd gave him a standing ovation, then started filing out as Sleepy Eyed John's band returned. I went backstage, where Elvis, his adrenaline flowing, was lit up like a Christmas tree.

"Let's go get some barbecue," he said. "How about Leonard's?"

"Sorry, man," said Bill. "One of my kids is sick. I gotta get home."

Scotty was putting away his guitar. "I was up late last night. I need some sleep."

Elvis turned to me. "Johnny? How about it?"

I thought of Lamont. "There's something I need to do. You go ahead."

"By myself?" said Elvis. "Hey, man, I need company."

"Next time," I said.

I got a ride with Scotty, who dropped me off a couple of blocks from Foote Homes.

"Why did we come here?" he asked.

"I need to see a friend," I told him. "Thanks for the lift."

He drove off, and I walked to Lamont's apartment. I knocked on the door.

"Lamont?" I said. "Are you okay?"

There was no answer. A lamp was on in the front room. I looked through the window to see if I could spot him.

"Hey, what are you doing?"

A tall Negro stood in the shadows, just off the porch. He was holding a big stick. My chest tightened, and I took a step back. Suddenly I realized he was the one who was scared.

I said, "I'm a friend of Lamont's. I was just checking on him."

The man lowered the stick. "Neighborhood's getting dangerous," he said. He looked me over one more time, then disappeared into the shadows.

I went back to the corner and caught the bus. Heading home, I thought about Lamont and wondered where he was. He was in no condition to be driving around. I hoped he had found a safe place to sleep it off.

A few other people were on the bus. All of them were Negroes, huddled in the back. Meanwhile I had the entire front to myself.

I remembered what the man with the stick had said. Maybe the neighborhood *was* getting dangerous. Maybe the most dangerous thing of all was what you took for granted, figuring that's the way it would always be.

When I woke up Sunday morning, my mother was sitting on the edge of the bed. "Johnny?"

"Yeah," I mumbled, still half-asleep.

"Something's happened. Lamont Turner was arrested last night."

I sat up straight. "What?"

"Irene called this morning. She said he's in jail."

Irene, the Chapmans' maid, always seemed to be the first to know things.

"What was it?" I asked. I imagined Lamont being hauled in and charged with public intoxication.

"He beat up Elvis Presley," she said.

I stared at her. I had heard her words, but they didn't make sense.

She said, "It was out at Clearpool, in an alley. You were at the concert, weren't you?"

"I left after the show. Everything was fine. Well, almost everything." I told her about the show, including what Lamont had done.

I shook my head, trying to sort through it all. "They're saying he beat up Elvis?"

She nodded. "They found Elvis in the alley. He had been attacked from behind, so he didn't see who it was. Then somebody told the police what had happened at the club, and they brought in Lamont."

"That's not right. He wouldn't do something like that."

"I'm afraid he would," she said.

"How do you know?"

She looked at her hands. "Well, it seems that he confessed."

"Confessed! He said that he did it?"

"Yes, according to Irene."

"That can't be," I said.

"Johnny, he's trouble."

"He's my friend."

"Don't say that!"

Suddenly I thought of something. "What about Elvis? Is he all right?"

"He's in the hospital. He was pretty beat up, but they say he'll be fine."

"I need to see him," I said.

She left the room, and I sank back into the pillow. It seemed that last night I had done all the wrong things. Lamont called for me, and I turned away. I went looking for him, but it was too late. Elvis wanted company, and I deserted him.

I had done all the wrong things, and my friends had paid for it. Elvis was in the hospital. Lamont was in jail.

I tried to imagine Lamont beating up Elvis. He'd probably been in a few fights. If I was honest, I had to admit that Lamont might have been mad enough to hit Elvis. But he would do it face-to-face, man-to-man, out in the open. He wouldn't sneak up behind him. I was sure of it.

But if Lamont didn't beat up Elvis, who did? If he really was innocent, why did he confess?

Everywhere I turned, there were questions. Why were we living on Belvedere Boulevard? Why did I like the blues? Did I really have a chance with Ruth Ann? Who were my friends? Why were they in trouble?

I hadn't been able to answer my own questions, but I could try to answer theirs. After what I had done—and hadn't done—it was the least I could do.

PART 3

Well, if I feel tomorrow
Like I feel today
I'm gonna pack my suitcase
And make my getaway
Lord I'm troubled, I'm all worried in mind
And I'm never bein' satisfied
And I just can't keep from cryin'

—Willie Dixon

CHAPTER TWENTY-ONE

The Criminal Court Building stood like a giant gravestone at the corner of Second and Washington in downtown Memphis. The courts were on the lower floors, and on the third floor was the jail, where Lamont was being held. When I went there Monday morning I found a man sitting at a metal desk, behind a nameplate that said W. EMMET ARMOUR, JAILOR.

"Can I help you?" he said, looking up from a magazine. He was a large man with sagging jowls and a bald head that was spotted with perspiration.

"I'd like to see Lamont Turner," I said.

He grunted. "Popular man. Already had some visitors." He handed me a clipboard. "Sign here."

I signed, just below some other names. Will Turner was at the top, followed by Lamont's mother. Below that was the neat signature of Arthur Chapman.

"Mr. Chapman was here?" I asked.

"He came Sunday morning. Didn't seem too happy, either."

I noticed another name below Arthur Chapman's. It was Nat D. Williams.

The jailor picked up a ring of keys and said, "Follow me."

The trip down the hallway was a short one, but I'd been dreading it just the same. I'd been planning to visit Lamont ever since Sunday, when I had found out what happened, but somehow other things kept coming up. I had stayed around the house that morning, then had spent most of the afternoon trying to reach Elvis. Finally, around supper time, his mother had answered the phone, saying that she and his father had been at the hospital all day. I asked if I could see Elvis, and she said it was probably better to wait a day or two. He had a concussion, and his face was pretty beat up. She didn't say so, but I got the feeling Elvis didn't want people to see him that way. By the time we finished talking I figured it was too late to visit Lamont, so I decided to go on Monday.

When Monday morning came, I took the bus to Sun Records. With Sam still on the road, the place was pretty quiet. Marion had heard about what happened to Elvis, and we talked about it for a while. She was surprised to hear that I didn't think Lamont did it. I asked for a few days off, and since things were slow, she agreed.

From there I got back on the bus and took it to the Criminal Court Building. I wondered what Lamont would do when I finally got there. After all, the last time I'd seen him, he had asked for help and I had turned away.

The jailor led me past a row of cells, all but one occupied by Negroes. It seemed odd in a city where half the people were white.

"I guess you heard what he did," said the jailor.

"Yes, sir."

"Mr. Chapman said to keep it quiet. Said don't tell the papers or nothin'. Anybody asks, we just say he was drunk."

"What's going to happen to him?" I asked.

"Hard to know. Could get some prison time. Maybe the chain gang."

I shuddered. I had seen chain gangs before, breaking up rocks in the quarry outside of town. It was hard to imagine Lamont shackled to a row of criminals, swinging a sledgehammer.

The jailor took me to a room that was bare except for a table and two chairs. He excused himself, and a moment later he led Lamont into the room.

"You got ten minutes," said the jailor. "I'll be right outside."

When I saw Lamont I thought he'd be angry, or at least resentful. I wasn't expecting indifference. He sat down in the chair, gazing ahead, his expression flat and lifeless.

I said, "Hi, Lamont."

"Hello," he said, barely looking at me.

I couldn't think of anything to say. Finally I blurted, "I'm sorry. I should have helped you at the club. Maybe it wouldn't have happened."

He didn't say anything. He just shook his head.

I said, "I came looking for you after they took you outside. The man at the door said you had left. I went to your apartment. I was worried about you. No one was there."

"It's all right," said Lamont.

"What happened?" I asked.

"It doesn't matter."

"Yes, it does. They might send you to prison."

Lamont looked up at me. "I waited for him in the alley and beat him up."

"He got hit from behind," I said. "He never saw who did it."

"It was me," said Lamont.

I studied his face. "I don't believe you."

He looked away. "I had too much to drink. I got mad. I broke the rule."

"Lamont," I said, "tell me the truth."

There was a glimmer of something in Lamont's eye. "Leave it alone, Johnny," he said in a quiet voice.

"You seem different."

Lamont raised his head. Suddenly I knew why he had been hiding his face. There was an expression of such anger and pain that I had to look away. It was white hot, like the glare of a spotlight. I had the feeling that if I looked right into it I might be blinded.

He said, "Stop it, now."

"Why are you doing this?" I asked.

"Go home," said Lamont. "Ain't no business of yours."

"Yes, it is. You're my friend."

Lamont called out, "Jailor."

The door opened, and the jailor entered.

"We're done," said Lamont. He got up to leave.

As the jailor led him out, I said, "I'm going to find out

what happened. I want to know who did it."

He looked up at me with an intensity that was frightening. "*I* did it. I did it with these fists. I made him bleed and I enjoyed it. You think you know me? You don't know me at all."

Outside the courthouse, I found that I was shaking. I sat down on a low wall. I thought about what Lamont had said. Maybe I didn't know him. Maybe, like the blues, there were things a white boy could never understand.

I wanted to find out. I needed to ask somebody, but I didn't know who. Then a name crossed my mind. I got up from the wall and headed down Second Street.

CHAPTER TWENTY-TWO

"Why do you want to see him?"

The woman stared at me from behind the front desk. I was in the offices of WDIA, the all-Negro radio station, on Union Avenue near Second. I had been surprised to see that the receptionist was white, along with several other people in the office. In fact, I might have thought I was at the wrong station if it hadn't been for the photos on the wall, showing the disc jockeys. I had heard all of them on my radio: Rufus Thomas, Willa Monroe, Gatemouth Moore, Ford Nelson, Moohah Williams, and Brother Theo "Bless My Bones" Wade. Above them all was a photo of the one I had come looking for, the man they called Nat D.

"It's about a friend of his," I said.

"Sorry," said the woman. "If I said yes to everybody who wanted to see him, we'd be packed in here like sardines."

Just then, a door behind her opened and a small, dark

man came out wearing a coat and tie, a hat, and the thickest glasses I'd ever seen.

"Mr. Williams," I said, "my name is Johnny Ross—"

"I know," he said.

"You know?"

He grinned. "Didn't they tell you? I know everybody."

Nat D. said something to the receptionist, then turned to me. "You like chili?"

"Yes sir, I do."

"Good. Let's have some lunch."

We walked up Union to Second Street, then headed down toward Beale.

I said, "Will Turner told me he knows you. He said he was a janitor at Washington High."

Nat D. chuckled. "Will Turner was never just a janitor. Oh, that's what it said on his door. But he was a lot more than that. He was the go-to man."

"Sir?"

"Need a hammer? Go to Will. Need a bandage? Go to Will. Need a friend when you're in trouble? Go to Will. When he left, things just weren't the same. The new janitor? Shoot, all he did was sweep and clean."

I thought of all the things Will did for Mr. Chapman. He was still the go-to man.

Nat D. said, "After Will left, he and I stayed in touch. He would come down to school and we'd visit. I was with him through the divorce. He kept me up to date on Lamont. It killed him to lose that boy. Later, he told me about the job with Chapman. Told me about you and your mother, too."

"He did?"

"You know, Johnny, he has a special feeling toward you."

We turned onto Beale Street, where Nat D. showed that he really did know everybody. He called off their names as we walked by, slapping their hands, clapping them on the shoulder. He made a special point of talking to his students, asking how their summer was going and saying he would see them in the fall.

A few doors down, he turned and headed up a stairway. At the top was a door with faded letters that read DOMINO LOUNGE. Inside, people were eating at rows of long, rickety tables. Beyond them was a platform with an upright piano on it, where a bent-over, gray-haired woman was pounding out the blues.

As we walked through the door, Nat D. called out, "Sunbeam! Where's my man?"

A large, friendly-faced man looked up from one of the tables. "Nat D.! Hey, y'all, look who's here."

There was a chorus of greetings from people around the room. Nat D. nodded back to them, then located a couple of chairs, and we sat down.

"What is this place?" I asked.

"The official name is the Domino Lounge, but everybody calls it Mitchell's. That's Sunbeam Mitchell over there. He's known as the godfather of Memphis musicians. If you're a musician and down on your luck or out of money, come by Mitchell's. Sunbeam'll give you a few bucks, feed you some chili, and send you on your way. Isn't that right, Sunbeam?"

I looked up. Sunbeam Mitchell was standing next to Nat D. "Lord, it's been a long time since you came around," said Mitchell. "What's it been—ten, twelve hours?" Mitchell laughed, wheezing heavily. "Nat D. here, he loves his chili. Why, just last week he stopped by for breakfast on the way to his radio show. Five o'clock in the morning. The place is full of musicians coming off their gigs, trying to offset their liquor with some chili, and here comes old Nat D. wanting chili for breakfast."

"I was out of gas, that's all," said Nat D. "I know if I come to Mitchell's, that's what I'll get. Gas."

Mitchell wheezed again, grinning with pleasure.

Nat D. said, "Sunbeam, I'd like to introduce you to a friend of mine, Johnny Ross."

Mitchell gazed down at me, and for just a moment I thought I saw a flicker of recognition in his face. Then it was gone. "Pleased to meet you, young man," he said.

He took our order and headed for the kitchen. I watched him go, then looked around. The woman was still pounding on the keyboard. It was a wonder the piano was still standing.

"Is this a nightclub?" I asked.

"Well, let's see," said Nat D. "It's a bar. It's a chili joint. It's a music venue. People come here when their gigs are over, eat some chili, catch up on the latest. They jam, compare licks, then jam some more. If they need something, they talk to Sunbeam."

A few minutes later Mitchell emerged from the kitchen carrying two bowls of chili, iced tea, and some crackers. He set them down in front of us.

"Eat up, boys. I got a fire extinguisher if you need it."

We dug in. The chili was hot, all right, somewhere between matches and a bonfire. But it was good. As I ate, I kept thinking about Lamont, shut up in that cell.

"I was over at the jail this morning," I said. "I saw your name on the sign-in sheet."

"It's a terrible thing about Lamont," he said.

"You really think he would do something like that?"

"I don't know. I've seen people do a lot of strange things. He says he did it. Told me right to my face. It doesn't seem right to me, but who knows?"

"Lamont was mad at Elvis," I said. "He accused him of stealing his moves—you know, the way Lamont shakes his legs on stage."

"Oh, yeah, I know about Lamont's moves. Everybody does, including that Presley kid."

I said, "All the trouble might have been my fault."

I told him what had happened at the Eagle's Nest, when I had denied knowing Lamont. Once I started confessing, I found I couldn't stop. It was something about the way he listened to me, with his kind eyes magnified behind the thick glasses. I described how I had gone to the garage the day before to see Will, and how Chapman had found us there.

I said, "I don't know exactly what I did, but Mr. Chapman was really mad at Will. Did Will say anything to you?"

"Not that I recall," said Nat D. I thought he might have looked away, but it was hard to tell through the thick glasses.

"Something's going on, Mr. Williams. There's something I don't know, and I mean to find out."

He looked up at me. "Son, you better watch yourself. You're treading on dangerous ground."

"What do you mean?"

"I mean Arthur Chapman. Everything the man does is dangerous. He's taken an interest in this thing."

"My mother says he's been good to us."

"Your mother's white. Talk to his Negro workers sometime. They'll tell you stories that'll make your skin crawl."

I said, "Then why do they work there?"

"Same as Will. It's a job. Things may be changing, though. These kids coming up, they'll have a better life, thanks to Mr. Brown."

"Who's he?" I asked.

"Brown versus the Board of Education? Don't tell me you never heard of it."

I shrugged.

"Man, what do they teach you in those white schools? You do know what the Supreme Court is, don't you?"

"Yes, sir."

"Well, three months ago they decided what we've known for years. So-called separate but equal schools for Negroes may be separate, but they sure aren't equal. No, sir. You should see Washington High. We've got a leaky roof, broken windows, books with missing pages. Meanwhile, over at Humes, they've got everything they want. It's not fair. I've been saying it for years. Now that the Supreme Court says it, people will start listening. They'll have to."

A few questions from me, and Nat D. had turned Mitchell's into a classroom. But he still hadn't answered the one question I had come for.

"Sir, I want to help Lamont," I said. "I think he's innocent. But he told me I'm wrong. He said I don't know him at all. I was wondering, what do you think? Did he do it? Did he beat up Elvis? Am I wasting my time?"

Nat D. didn't answer for a while. Finally he said, "Johnny, if you believe in someone, it's never a waste of time."

"Do you think I could ever know him? Are we really that different?"

He looked at me thoughtfully. "Oh, yeah, you're different," he said. "You sure are."

CHAPTER TWENTY-THREE

The cuts and bruises and swollen jaw were new, but underneath, it was the same old Elvis with the same shy grin.

"How are you feeling?" I asked.

"Better. At least they didn't beat up my voice."

Scotty said, "I figured we should go ahead and practice. We've got the Eagle's Nest on Saturday."

Monday afternoon I'd gotten a call from Elvis, saying he was out of the hospital and would be rehearsing that night at the cleaners. I had hurried over after supper, eager to see him and find out more about what had happened. When I arrived, Elvis, Scotty, and Bill were setting up. Dixie was there too, staying close by Elvis, bringing him things when he asked for them.

"You think it's safe to go back to the Eagle's Nest?" I asked Scotty.

"Hey, man, the guy's in jail. It's fine."

I turned to Elvis. "What happened that night? Do you remember anything?"

"Nothing much. After you all left, I headed for my car. I heard a noise behind me, but before I could turn, somebody hit me over the head and started pounding away. I guess I blacked out. Next thing I knew, I was in the hospital."

"Did you get a look at him?" I asked.

"Naw, man. He came up behind me. It was dark."

"Dark," said Bill. "Yeah, that's the word for it, all right." He elbowed Scotty, who just shook his head.

Elvis looked over at Bill. "It's not funny, man. They're holding Lamont Turner."

"Well, of course they are," said Bill. "Did you hear the way he screamed at you in the club? They had to hold him back."

Elvis said, "All I know is, Lamont's a bluesman. He's a musician. I can't believe he would do that."

"You would if you'd heard him," said Bill. "He accused you of stealing the music. He said you copied his moves."

"That's not true," said Elvis. "What I do when I'm singing—it's not planned. It's just the way I am. You know that, right?"

I said, "If he didn't do it, who did?"

"I don't know," said Elvis.

"Honey, you want another Coke?" asked Dixie. She was hanging on his arm, watching everything he did.

Elvis said yes. When she brought him the Coke, he leaned down and kissed her. As he did, I noticed a bandage on the back of his head.

"Is that where they hit you?" I asked.

He nodded. "The first time, anyway. That's what knocked me out. The doctor said they used something big and heavy."

I looked more closely. The bandage, covering a big gash, was on the right side of his head. "Something big and heavy? That's what the doctor said?"

"That's right," said Elvis.

I remembered what Lamont had told me earlier that morning. He didn't mention anything big and heavy. He said he had used his fists. I thought of something else. The bruises on Elvis's face, like the bandage on the back of his head, were on the right side. But Lamont was left-handed.

The next day I took the bus downtown to the police station. The man at the front desk recognized me.

"Back again, huh? Want to see Sergeant Linebaugh?"

I shook my head. "This is about Lamont Turner. He was arrested Saturday night."

"What are you," said the man, grinning down at me, "some kind of junior crime fighter?"

"Can I talk to the person handling the case? I have some information."

"Oh, really?"

"Could you just check?" I said. "It's important."

"Look, sonny, we're pretty busy around here. If you want to write down the information, I'll be happy to pass it on."

"Maybe I should take it to the newspapers," I said.

The man chuckled. "Yeah, maybe you should."

"I think they'd like some news about Elvis Presley."

"Presley? Did you say Presley?"

"Yeah, somebody beat him up. Didn't you hear?"

I turned to leave.

"Now, hold on," said the man. Fumbling through the notes on his desk, he picked one out and scanned it. "Wait here. I'll just be a minute."

He went into the back and returned a moment later with a short, squat officer with sandy hair and freckles.

"This is Sergeant Cross," said the man. "He wants to talk with you."

Sergeant Cross took me into a side room and closed the door. He said, "The Presley family wants us to keep this quiet. I'm sure you understand."

I understood more than he thought. It wasn't the family who wanted to keep it quiet. It was Arthur Chapman. The jailor had said so. Maybe it was because Lamont Turner was his employee. Maybe it was something else.

I introduced myself, saying I knew Lamont and Elvis.

"The thing is," I explained, "Lamont wouldn't do this. I know he wouldn't."

Sergeant Cross gave me a funny look. "Wouldn't do it? He was screaming at Presley. He was drunk. An hour later, Presley got beaten up. Seems pretty obvious to me. Besides, Turner confessed. He told us he did it."

"That's what he told me, too. But he claimed he used his fists. The doctor said Elvis was hit by something big and heavy."

"This is what you wanted to tell me?"

"There's more," I said. "All the injuries were on the right side. But Lamont's left-handed."

"So?" said Cross.

"He's innocent. He's not that kind of person."

"Well, that's very touching, but you're wrong."

"He didn't do it, I'm sure."

Cross said, "Son, let me give you some advice. Forget about this thing. I don't know how you got involved, but you're in over your head. You hear me?"

Leaving the station, I had no idea what to do next. I thought of Elvis at Overton Park, in my living room, backstage at the Eagle's Nest. It reminded me of something, but I couldn't remember what. Some picture, some fragment floated by, and I couldn't reel it in. And then it came to me.

I took a bus to K's. I ordered a burger and Coke at the window, then sat at a table and ate. The waitresses bustled around, going out to the cars and back again. I wanted to get Ruth Ann's attention, but every time I saw her she seemed to be looking the other way. Finally I called out to her. She glanced around nervously, then came over.

She said, "My boss doesn't like us visiting with the customers."

"Is something wrong?" I asked.

"I'm sorry. I can't talk now."

I said, "This will just take a minute."

Not sure how to start, I took a sip of my Coke. I must have swallowed wrong, because suddenly I started coughing.

"Are you okay?" she asked.

"Fine," I said, "I'm fine."

I was croaking like a frog, but I didn't dare stop. Otherwise I'd never work up the nerve to ask the question.

"I was just wondering," I said. "On Saturday night I saw you backstage at the Eagle's Nest. What were you doing there?"

There was a blank expression on her face. "I don't know. I think I was with Trey."

I said, "He wasn't there. You were by yourself."

She gazed off into the distance. "I was meeting a friend," she said.

I swallowed. "Were you with Elvis?"

She shook her head, a strange look in her eye.

"What happened, Ruth Ann?"

She looked at me, as beautiful as ever. This time, though, there was a kind of sadness I hadn't seen before.

"I have to go," she said, and abruptly turned away.

CHAPTER TWENTY-FOUR

When I got home, Trey Chapman's Cadillac convertible was parked in front of his house. I climbed inside and sat in the passenger seat. It wasn't long before the big front doors to the house swung open.

"Hey, what are you doing?" yelled Trey. He was wearing blue jeans and a white T-shirt with a pack of cigarettes rolled up in the sleeve.

I didn't say anything. I was nervous, but I needed to talk with him, and I didn't want to do it in his house.

"You! Hey! Johnny!"

When I didn't answer, he shook his head and came stomping out to the car. He reached in and grabbed my arm.

"Look," I said, "I'm sorry about this."

"You'll be sorrier in a minute."

I said, "It's about Ruth Ann."

He stopped. "What about her?"

"Can we talk? Someplace private?"

"Tell me here," he said.

"Sorry, I can't."

He studied me, then let go of my arm and pulled some keys out of his pocket. "Let's go," he said.

We drove up Belvedere Boulevard, going slowly. Trey lit up a cigarette, placed the pack on the seat, and gazed at the mansions as we passed by. They were huge, like his father's place, some of them more like cathedrals than homes. As we cruised through the neighborhood, I realized it was Trey's way of telling me, without words, that we might not be in his house but we were still on his turf.

"What do you want?" he asked finally.

"I went out with Ruth Ann," I said.

His fist came from nowhere, catching me square in the mouth. My head bounced back and hit the door. Bright lights flashed.

Trey yanked the wheel sideways and pulled over, his eyes wild. Grabbing me, he shoved me against the door. He brought back his fist to hit me again.

"So did Elvis," I said.

Trey stopped. He peered àt me.

"We need to talk," I said.

I pulled a handkerchief from my pocket and wiped my mouth. It came away with blood on it.

Trey's hands opened and closed. "This better be good," he said.

I'd always been afraid of Trey hitting me. Now that it had happened, I was surprised to find that it wasn't really so bad. Sure, it had hurt. But other things hurt more.

"I went to the Eagle's Nest on Saturday night," I said. "I saw Ruth Ann backstage."

He eyed me warily. "I took her backstage to see Elvis. I thought she might like it. You know girls."

"She was by herself," I said. "You weren't around."

His gaze darted around the car. It came to rest on the pack of cigarettes. He shook one out and lit it. Leaning back in the driver's seat, he inhaled deeply.

I said, "I saw Lamont Turner yesterday."

Trey shook his head. "That's sad, isn't it? You give a boy a chance, and he ruins it all in one night."

"He was drunk," I said. "But I don't think he did anything."

"Man, he beat up Elvis Presley."

"I'm not so sure."

"Maybe you didn't hear," said Trey. "He confessed."

"I know."

Trey held his cigarette out the window and tapped off the ashes. As I watched him, something in the backseat caught my eye. It was the baseball bat. It was well used. It was big and heavy.

"Do you always carry that bat with you?" I asked.

"Huh? Who cares? I don't know."

My heart was hammering. "I don't think Lamont did it. I think it was someone else."

Trey said, "Look, none of this matters. Turner confessed. End of story."

I didn't say anything. I just watched him.

Trey straightened his shoulders. "How long have you lived at our house?"

"Fifteen years," I said. "Longer for my mom."

"Nice place, isn't it?"

"Why are you asking?" I said.

"Just curious."

He smiled. He had delivered a threat, as ominous as the bat in the backseat.

Dabbing my mouth with the handkerchief, I thought about what had happened at the Eagle's Nest on Saturday night. I imagined Trey arriving there, looking for Ruth Ann. Maybe he had seen her with Elvis. Maybe someone had told him. However he found out, he had ended up in a dark alley behind the club.

Trey Chapman had beaten up Elvis and had probably used the bat to do it. But it left a question unanswered. If Lamont was innocent, how had Trey convinced him to take the blame?

"Turner's guilty," said Trey. "Why else would he confess?"

I said, "Maybe something else is going on." I studied him for a long time, my throat dry. "What is it, Trey? What's going on?"

He shook his head. "Drop it, Johnny."

"Why should I?"

"Don't push this," he said. "Things aren't the way they seem."

"Lamont's my friend. I want to help him."

"Believe me, you don't want any part of this."

"Why not?" I asked.

"If you knew the truth, you wouldn't go near him. You'd stay as far away as you could."

I thought about Lamont sitting in jail. I thought about him on the chain gang.

"I went to the police station today," I said. "I met the man handling Lamont's case. His name is Sergeant Cross. Maybe I'll go back there and talk to him."

Trey looked over, as if sizing me up.

"Do me a favor," he said. "Don't go to the police. Don't talk to anyone. Don't do anything until you know the answer to one simple question."

"What's that?" I asked.

He took a drag from his cigarette, squinting through the smoke. Then he flipped it out the window.

"Who's your father, Johnny?"

Trey let me out in front of the house and drove off. As I went inside, I tried to picture the man I had always thought of as my father. His name was Carl Ross. My mother had told me he had left when she was pregnant and had gone to Detroit, looking for work in the auto plants. That was about all I knew.

By supper time my lip was swollen. I told my mother I'd run into a door. I knew she didn't believe me. After supper she decided to make boiled custard, my favorite dessert.

She went to her card file and pulled out her mother's recipe. Boiled custard was a rich, sweet drink, like eggnog, only thicker. She made it in her double boiler, nursing it slowly and carefully.

As always, she brought out some of Granny's crystal— an engraved pitcher and two goblets. She filled the pitcher with custard, carefully poured some into the goblets, then placed the pitcher and goblets in front of us on the kitchen table and sat down.

I sipped the custard. It took me back to the time when my grandmother was alive. She knew what had happened when I was born, I was sure. Maybe she knew more about me than I did.

Using my finger, I traced the lines on the crystal pitcher. I said, "This afternoon I talked with Trey, and he asked me a question. I wondered if you could answer it for me."

"I'll try."

I studied the pitcher, then looked up at her. "Who's my father?"

She blinked several times, quickly. "I've told you that, Johnny. His name is Carl Ross."

"Why did he leave when you were pregnant? What kind of man would do that?"

She said, "He was a good person. I'm sure he had his reasons."

I thought about the life my mother and I led. I thought of the house where we lived and the good deal we had on the rent. I had often wondered why we stayed there.

"You know," I said, "one thing I've noticed is that when couples break up, the father usually stays close by, so he can see the children. It seems strange that my father didn't."

She fingered her goblet nervously. "Johnny, this is pointless. You're only going to upset yourself."

I thought about my mother's work. She was good at what she did. She had a lot of responsibility but didn't get paid very much. Why didn't she look for another job?

Maybe I knew the answer. Lamont thought he knew.

What was it he had said? *How long has she been with Chapman? Say, fifteen years?*

Maybe the answer was that Arthur Chapman wanted my mother nearby so he could keep an eye on her. He wanted to keep an eye on her son, too.

His son.

It would explain a lot of things, including why Trey had asked me who my father was. Trey thought that if I discovered I was a Chapman, I would naturally take his side against Lamont.

I took a sip of custard and watched my mother. She had found a loose thread on her dress and was picking at it.

I said, "I've been thinking about my father. I think he had a good reason for leaving. Maybe it was simple. He wasn't my father."

"Stop it," said my mother. "Stop it now."

"I know your secret," I said.

Watching her, I thought about how it must have been. Carl Ross was busy with his job. My mother wanted attention, and she got it—at work. Maybe she began staying late. Before long, she was pregnant. At first Carl assumed he was the father. Then somehow he learned the truth. Maybe he found a clue and confronted her. Maybe he caught them together. However it happened, he couldn't live with it. My whole life, I'd been wondering what kind of man would leave his wife when she was pregnant. Now I knew: a man whose wife was about to have someone else's child.

"So, you know why he left," said my mother.

"Yeah. It took a while, but I figured it out."

"You know everything?"

"You should have told me, Mom. I'm not a little boy anymore."

Her shoulders sagged. She buried her face in her hands. "Johnny, I am so sorry."

"Sorry! Is that all you can say?"

"We can't tell anyone, Johnny. They can't find out. I promised."

"Why?" I asked.

"It was his choice," she said. "He made it a long time ago. We agreed never to tell anyone, including you." She smiled sadly. "Of course, we left one clue. But no one's ever noticed it."

"What was it?"

She said, "Your name."

"Johnny?" I asked.

"Your real name, Johnson. It's your father's middle name—William Johnson Turner."

CHAPTER TWENTY-FIVE

I stared at her. A look of horror spread slowly across her face. "You didn't know? You said you knew everything."

I didn't hear her. I was back in Will's house, looking at the picture of his mother. He had said that her name was Hattie Mae Johnson. Johnson was her maiden name, and it became his middle name. Now it was my name.

At the time I had thought there was something familiar about her, but I couldn't think of what it was. Now I knew. I had seen a face similar to hers every day of my life, whenever I looked in the mirror.

How could I have missed it? I had her name and her face. Hattie Mae Johnson was my grandmother.

I thought of the times I had wondered about my father. All along he had been right outside my door, planting flowers, waxing the car.

"I thought you knew," said my mother, almost pleading. "Otherwise I wouldn't have told you. Not in a million years. Who did you think it was?"

"Arthur Chapman," I said.

Her hands flew to her mouth. "Mr. Chapman? God, no."

"Will Turner is my father," I said dully.

"Yes," she said in a small voice.

"But I'm white."

"That part was a surprise," she said. "None of the rest was. It was as natural as could be."

She hugged herself, rocking back and forth, shivering. "I loved music, and I loved to have fun. Carl didn't. I had a wild streak, and I noticed Will. He was warm. He was exciting. He had a life outside of work, in his neighborhood, on Beale Street. So we started seeing each other. At first it was hard for me. I was brought up in the South, where you just didn't do that. But Will was so patient and kind. When I got pregnant, Carl knew right away that it wasn't his child. By that time he and I weren't having relations. He asked me who the father was, and finally I told him. So he left."

It made perfect sense. After all, his wife was involved with another man. The man was a Negro. And she was going to have the man's baby. The reason Carl Ross had left was as clear, as plain, as brutal as Memphis itself.

My mother said, "Will and I needed money, so while I was pregnant we decided to tell Mr. Chapman it was Carl's baby. That way I could keep working. Mr. Chapman didn't know about Will and me. Nobody but Carl did, and he was gone. Of course, we thought that when the baby arrived, everyone would find out. But the day you were born, you came out white. I've never been so shocked in my life.

"I didn't know what to do. Neither did Will. But I could see that he was thinking about it. That night he told me his idea. It seems that what happened with you isn't so unusual.

There are lots of people who have a Negro parent and look white. Some of them decide to live as white people. We just don't hear much about it, because they keep it a secret. It's called 'passing.' We decided you would pass. We would say what we'd been saying all along—that you were Carl's baby. That's what we told everyone."

"Even me," I said.

"Especially you."

"It was Will's idea?"

She nodded. "From the beginning. He's stuck by it all these years."

"But he's a Negro. Why would he want me to be white?"

As soon as I asked the question, I knew the answer. I had just said it myself. He was a Negro. That had been his life, and he didn't want it to be mine.

"Your father is a very generous man," said my mother.

"So," I said, "what will we do?"

She straightened up and wiped her eyes. "The same thing we've been doing for the last fifteen years. We'll just keep going."

"You still want to keep it a secret?"

"Of course," she said.

"But it's a lie."

She cocked her head. "Johnny, we have no choice."

"What about Will?"

She said, "It was his idea. He's got a lot invested in it. Don't let him down."

"Maybe I should tell people the truth."

"What truth?" she asked. "What would you say?"

"I'm not white. I never was."

"Aren't you? Your skin is white. You were raised white. People see you as white. What else is there?"

There was a mirror over the table. I looked at myself. One moment I was white. The next moment I wasn't. The images flickered back and forth. I squinted, trying to make sense of them.

I turned back to my mother and said, "Who am I?"

She leaned across the table. Gripping my shoulders, she gazed at me with a look so fierce I almost staggered.

"You're Johnny Ross. You're white. Do you understand?"

A feeling started in my chest and began to spread. It was like heat, as if something inside me was burning. It grew hotter and hotter. I got to my feet. I paced beside the table, trying to push the feeling down, but there was no stopping it. My face was hot. My fists throbbed. I raised them into the air and brought them down onto the table, hard. The crystal jumped and swayed.

"Lies!" I said. "All of it! Your job is a lie. This house is a lie. This neighborhood, this city, everything."

I picked up a goblet. "Look at this. We pretend to be so fancy, like everyone else on Belvedere Boulevard. But we're not. We're the hired help. Like Will. Like Lamont. This is just another lie."

I raised the goblet over my head and threw it to the floor. It smashed into pieces.

My mother was crying.

I said, "You're always telling me we shouldn't keep secrets. But it's all you've ever done."

"I was trying to help you."

"Well, I didn't ask for it. And I don't want it. I don't want any of it."

Reaching out, I raked the pitcher off the table, along with the other goblet. They fell to the floor with a crash.

"I have to go," I said hoarsely.

"Where?"

"I don't know."

I stumbled across the room and out the door. It was still light outside. The heat was suffocating. It pressed against me from all sides, closing in. I started walking.

Behind me I heard my mother call, "Johnny, come back!"

I didn't stop. I didn't break stride. I just walked, hearing my mother's voice, seeing Will's face. They floated in front of me like a bad dream. The clouds were low and menacing. Crickets and cicadas and tree frogs screamed in the distance.

I glanced down at my hands. They seemed to be white. If you looked more closely, maybe they were a darker shade. I had never thought color was important, but now I realized I'd been wrong. Trey Chapman knew how important it was. He used his skin color like a hammer. For a few moments I had actually thought he was my brother. Now I knew the truth. I had a brother, but it wasn't Trey Chapman. It was Lamont Turner.

I found my way to the bus stop and took a bus downtown. When I got off, I headed toward Beale Street.

The street was crowded, as usual. But the stores and clubs looked different. They weren't dark and mysterious, the way they had seemed before. They looked shabby and worn. The paint was peeling. Windows were broken. Doors needed repair. There were potholes in the street. The people were tired. Their steps were slow. Their faces were sad. The faces looked like Hattie Mae Johnson. They looked like me.

I got back on the bus and didn't get off. I rode from one end of Memphis to the other and back again, looking out the window, watching the passengers, wondering what it was like to sit in the colored section. I pictured Lamont in the jail cell, Elvis at the Eagle's Nest, my mother at work, my mother with Will Turner. It was like a strange, fevered dream. The air clung to me, hot and wet. People got on and off, but I just sat there sweating, staring into the darkness.

CHAPTER TWENTY-SIX

When I woke up, it was still dark. I rolled over, and my shoulder hit something. There was a loud crash. Things clattered and bumped and jangled. I thought it would never end, and then, finally, it did. I sat up.

Where was I?

Suddenly I remembered. Climbing to my feet, I fumbled for a light switch and turned it on. I was in the recording studio at Sun Records. The thing I had rolled into was a drum set in the corner. It lay at my feet, the bass drum upended and the cymbal upside down.

After riding the bus the night before, I didn't want to go back to my house. I knew my mother would be inside, waiting for me. I needed to be someplace else, a place where people didn't care if you were black or white. So I headed home.

When Sam had left on his trip, he had given me a key to Sun Records. I went around behind the little brick building and let myself in. I got a Coca-Cola from the machine, sat by the drums, and thought for a long time. Sometime late in the night I must have fallen asleep on the floor.

I checked my watch. It was seven o'clock in the morning. Remembering the bathroom off to one side, I went in, splashed some water on my face, and looked in the mirror over the sink. I was staring at a stranger.

A key jiggled in the lock, and the studio door opened. A shadowy figure entered, wearing old slacks and a sweaty undershirt. His clothes were dirty, and his hair was messed up. When he turned, the light struck his face.

"Sam?" I said.

He jumped back. "Johnny? What are you doing here?"

"You look terrible," I said.

"Same back at you. What happened to your mouth?"

I didn't want to tell Sam what had happened, so I made up a story about some kid in the neighborhood. He seemed to buy it. I said, "I've been coming in early some mornings to clean up. Marion said it was okay."

Sam glanced over at the drum set, which looked as if someone had planted a bomb under it. "You're doing a great job," he said.

I asked why he was so dirty. He told me that when he was driving in from Georgia the night before, the car had broken down. Sam, always good with machines, had crawled under the car and managed to fix it, but by the time he got back to Memphis it was morning. He had a session scheduled with Elvis that day and had decided to come straight to the studio to clean up and get ready.

I started to tell him about Elvis getting beat up, but it

turned out he already knew. Marion had reached him on the road and given him the news. Sam, after learning Elvis was fine, had agreed it would be best for everyone if the incident was kept quiet.

Sam changed clothes, and we got ready for the session. Elvis, Scotty, and Bill arrived a little bit later. Somebody had decided that Elvis should try singing a ballad called "Tomorrow Night," but it didn't seem to work very well. On about the fourth try I found myself losing interest. It was partly because of the song and the way Elvis was singing it, but mostly it was me.

I'd been hanging around Sun Records all summer, imagining I was part of it all. But Sam, Marion, Elvis, the musicians—they were doing the important work. I was pushing a broom. Sam called me a gofer, but I knew better. My job was the same one held by Negroes all over Memphis, the same one held by Will Turner when he had worked at Washington High. I was a janitor.

As Elvis tried the song one more time, I slipped out the door. As much as I'd wanted it to be true, the people at Sun Records weren't my family. Lamont was.

I wondered how much he knew and what Will had told him. I thought of him in jail, and my mind returned to the question I'd asked the previous night. Why did Lamont confess? Whatever it was, he had decided it was worth going to prison over. What could possibly be that important? Other than Lamont, I knew of just one person who could answer that question.

* * *

When I arrived, Trey was sitting on the front steps of his house, smoking.

"Hello, Johnny," he said.

"Hello."

"You don't look so good. Your lip's puffed up, and you're sweating like a pig. No offense."

I said, "I know what happened."

"Pardon me?"

"I know what happened at the Eagle's Nest."

"Oh, really?" He tapped the ash from his cigarette onto the step. "Then why don't you tell me?"

"You beat up Elvis. You left him in the alley. Then you blackmailed Lamont Turner to make him confess."

"Lamont Turner's a tough boy," said Trey. "How would I do that?"

"That's what I'd like to know. What did you tell him, Trey?"

Trey shook his head. "You're dreaming, Johnny. It's all in your mind."

I said, "I think it had something to do with Will's secret."

"Secret? What are you talking about?"

I took a deep breath. My voice quivered as I spoke. "Will Turner is my father. I found out last night."

Trey took a drag from his cigarette and blew a smoke ring. It twirled in the air above him. He smiled. "Then I'd say you'd better keep your mouth shut."

"I'm going to the police," I said.

"And what will you tell them?"

The smoke ring wobbled and drifted apart.

"What do you mean?" I asked.

"Maybe you should practice it right here. Like you'll say it at the police station. Like you'll say it to the newspapers."

"Newspapers?"

"Go ahead, Johnny. Practice: I'm a Negro."

I took a step back.

Trey put out his cigarette and got to his feet, advancing on me. "Say it. I'm a Negro." I moved back. He bore down on me. "I'm a Negro. I'm a Negro. What's wrong, Johnny? You don't like that? I'm a Negro. I'm a nigra. I'm a nigger." His voice was like steel. "Say it. I'm a nigger. *Say it!*"

I turned and ran, across the driveway and down the street. Behind me, Trey Chapman laughed.

CHAPTER TWENTY-SEVEN

An hour later I was downtown, in front of radio station WDIA. I went inside. The same woman was sitting at the front desk. This time she recognized me.

"You want to see Nat D.?" she said. "He just finished up his show. I think he's still here."

She led me down the hall to a little office at the foot of the stairs. Inside, books were jammed into shelves and stacked on the floor. The walls were covered with newspaper clippings. In the middle of it all was a rickety desk, and at the desk sat Nat D. Williams.

He looked up at me and smiled. "Hey, Johnny." He nodded at the woman, and she left.

"Have a seat," he said, clearing off a chair. "You don't look so good."

I touched my mouth, but he shook his head. "I don't mean your lip. You want something? A glass of water?"

"No, thanks," I said.

"You look worried. You know what I always say. Worrying is just like a rocking chair. Lots of movement, but you ain't getting nowhere."

I tried to smile. "I'm not sure why I'm here," I said.

"That's all right," said Nat D. "You just sit and relax."

He gazed at me through his thick glasses, his eyes big and warm.

Finally I said, "You were good friends with Will Turner. Did he tell you about him and my mother?"

Nat D. was silent for a moment. Then he said, "Yes."

"Did he tell you about me?"

"Yes, Johnny, he did."

For some reason it made me angry. "Why didn't you say anything? You knew about it, and you didn't tell me."

"Wasn't my place. That was for Will to decide." He heaved a sigh. "How did you find out?"

I told him. He listened. Then he leaned back in his chair. "You know, Johnny, we've been waiting for you. We've been waiting a long time."

"We?"

"A few of us down on Beale. Two or three close friends of Will's."

"Is Sunbeam Mitchell one of them?"

Nat D. smiled. "You're quick. Will always said you were."

"I'm a Negro. I'm black." I don't know why I said it. It just popped out.

"Hey, man, we're all black. We're all white. Just like you. Only difference is, most people don't know it."

207

"I've always heard that one drop of black blood makes you a Negro."

Nat D. laughed. "Black blood? What's that? It's red, man. Just like yours. Just like Dwight D. Eisenhower's. Dwight and me? For all I know, we could be cousins."

"Dwight D. Eisenhower? The president?"

"Listen here. Abe Lincoln's my daddy. Booker T. Washington's his. We breathe the same air. We work the same fields. We're two sides of the same coin. Black or white. Heads or tails. You call it."

"I don't know," I said. "I feel different."

"Think of it as a club. Now you're a member."

"I guess I always was."

"So," said Nat D., "you know who your father is. What are you going to do?"

I knew he would ask that question. I'd been dreading it.

"You're going to hate me," I said.

"I'm too old to hate."

"I'm sorry, Mr. Williams. I've been thinking about it a lot. I'm not going to tell anybody. I'm going to keep it a secret."

He took off his glasses and wiped them with a handkerchief, then put them back on. "When Will first talked to me about this, he said the same thing. I'll tell you what I told him. You're wrong. There's too many secrets in the world. Set 'em free. Air 'em out. Tell the truth."

"I can't."

"Yes, you can. You're stronger than you think."

It reminded me of Lamont. He was strong. And he was in trouble.

"Can I ask you something, Mr. Williams? Does this have anything to do with Lamont being in jail?"

"I don't know," said Nat D. "Have you asked Will?"

"I haven't really talked to him."

Nat D. eyed me. "You'll have to eventually, you know."

"Is Lamont going to prison?" I asked.

"In Memphis? For beating up a white man? I should say so."

"That's awful."

"Johnny, go see Will."

I said, "I don't think I can."

"You have no idea what he's been through. You know how many times he's wanted to put his arm around you, comfort you, tell you everything's okay? All he could do was stand by and watch. Couldn't say anything. Couldn't even touch you."

I thought of Will in the garden, watching me day after day, year after year. There had been something in his eyes, some look, some feeling. Now I knew what it was. It was love.

I stood up to go. "Thanks for talking to me."

As I walked down the hall, I turned back to look at him. He was watching me. I guess he'd been watching for a long time.

I found Will sitting on his front porch swing, moving back and forth, back and forth. Somehow it fit. He was always the same, always there, always waiting.

"Hello," I said.

He looked up at me, his expression impossible to read.

I said, "We need to talk."

"Go ahead."

I didn't know how to start. My stomach was churning. I'd been wondering about my father for my whole life, and now he was sitting in front of me. The weight of fifteen years pressed down on me, along with guilt for what I had decided to do.

"I spoke to my mother last night. I had this crazy idea. I thought Mr. Chapman was my father."

Will blinked. For just a moment I saw something in his face. It looked like pain.

"What did she say?" he asked.

"She misunderstood me. She thought I was talking about someone else. So she told me what happened."

Will was silent for the longest time.

"I found out, Will. I know all about it."

His eyes darted back and forth, from me to the front steps. I wondered if he wanted to leave. I know I wanted to—at least, part of me did. Another part wanted to walk over and put my arms around him.

I said, "You're my father. I'm your son."

He sat there, stunned. After fifteen years, it was over. The secret was out.

My legs felt shaky, so I sat down on the steps. I told him what I had learned and how. When I finished, he leaned forward.

"You know," he said, "you can't tell anybody."

Thinking about it later, I wondered if it was self-defense. Maybe he sensed something in my voice, realized what I had decided, and couldn't bear to hear me say it. So he had said it for me.

"You can have a good life," said Will.

"A white life."

He nodded. "There are days when it's all right being a Negro. You wake up and sit in the sunshine and thank God for all of it. Maybe you see a mother and her baby out for a stroll. You start to smile and tip your hat, and she crosses to the other side of the street to avoid you. At the park, you look for a bathroom, and a sign says WHITE ONLY. At work, you push a broom while some cracker half your age sits in a fancy office. No, man. You have a choice. You need to be white."

"What about the blues?" I said. "I love the blues."

He eyed me. "Don't get any ideas, now. You say the wrong thing and this could all come tumbling down. I'd lose my job. Your mother would lose hers. You'd be kicked out of your house. You'd have to leave your school and go to Washington High. It almost happened once. I don't want it to happen now."

"Almost happened? What do you mean?"

"Didn't she tell you?" He studied my face. "No, I don't believe she did."

He settled back in the swing. I sat down on the steps.

"When you were born," said Will, "we decided not to tell anyone I was the father. You know that part. It wasn't easy, but in a way we had a nice little setup. For the first few months, your mother did the bookkeeping at home. I stayed on as gardener. At night I would sneak in with her, and we'd spend the evening playing with you.

"One night Chapman found us there. He saw me holding you, and he knew. He said we had twenty-four hours to get out.

"I went to see him the next day. I asked him to reconsider. Did he really want to lose his bookkeeper? I knew he could find a new gardener, but I had an ace up my sleeve. Chapman loved his cars, and Carl Ross had always kept them in perfect condition. Ever since Ross had left, though, the cars had been a problem. They weren't maintained. They weren't driven right. No one that Chapman hired was any good.

"What he didn't know was that when I was younger, I'd been a mechanic. My brother owned a garage, and I could repair anything he brought me. I offered to spend the day working on Chapman's cars, and if he liked what I did I'd stay on as his driver. Well, by sundown those cars were gleaming, and they ran like a top. He took my offer, and that's the way it's been ever since. It was all because of one thing—Arthur Chapman loves cars more than he hates Negroes."

Fifteen years after Chapman accepted his offer, I could still see the pride in Will's face. He had stared down Arthur Chapman, and he had won.

"Chapman kept us on," said Will, "but there was one condition. I had to break it off with your mother and stay away from both of you. I could watch you from a distance, but I couldn't be involved in any way. If I broke that rule, he would tell everyone the truth, and all of us would have to leave."

I said, "That day when Mr. Chapman saw us, he asked you to come to his office. What did he tell you?"

"He said it was my last chance. One more slip and we were gone. All of us. You know the worst part? He smiled.

He had all the power. I was helpless, and he enjoyed every minute of it. It reminded me of something that happened when I was your age. I saw a lynching. I hid in the bushes and watched while they tied a rope around a man's neck and hung him up to die, just for being a Negro. The people who strung up that man, they were smiling too.

"After I talked with Chapman, I went home and got drunk—hard, hard, stinking drunk. It had been bad enough losing you the first time, but to have you at my house, to see you with your brother, and then lose you again? That was too much."

I said, "Lamont got drunk too. You know why? He showed me the newspaper. Those boys got released. The ones who burned the cross. It made him crazy. He had a bottle. He took it with him to Clearpool. That's why he got in trouble. When he saw Elvis doing his moves, he couldn't take it anymore."

"He was a fool. He beat up a white man."

"No, he didn't," I said.

Will's head jerked up, and he stared at me. "Lamont confessed. He said he beat up Elvis Presley. Why would he do that if it wasn't true?"

Looking at Will, I had an idea.

"You went to see him that night," I said. "I saw your name on the clipboard."

"That's right. He called me."

"What did he say when you got there?"

Will said, "Now that you mention it, it was kind of strange. He didn't want to talk. Didn't want a lawyer. He just asked me a question."

"What was it?" I asked.

I could tell Will was embarrassed, but he told me anyway. "'Did you ever have an affair with a white woman?'"

"What did you say?"

"Yes."

"Did you tell him who it was?"

Will shook his head. "He didn't want to hear it. I wouldn't have told him anyway. No use having more people know."

I stopped pacing and looked at him. I saw someone who was honest but whose feelings were closely guarded. Will was good at building fences and recognizing those that others had built. It was a quality that may have saved my life, or at least life as I knew it. It also blinded him to certain things.

"What did he say after that?" I asked.

"He said, 'I did it. I beat up Elvis Presley.' He told the jailor, and the jailor made some phone calls. That was about it."

I said, "I noticed Lamont's mother signed in after you did."

"I didn't see her," said Will. "It must have been after I left."

"The two of them are pretty close, aren't they?"

"Always were. Not like him and me. We never connected."

I said, "I wonder why he didn't call her first."

"Huh?"

"His mother. If they're so close, why did he call you? Then, when you got there, why did he ask that question?"

Will looked past me, thinking.

I said, "Who knew that you were my father?"

"Me. Your mother. Chapman."

"There was someone else," I said. "I'm not sure how he found out, but he knew."

I turned to leave.

"Lamont didn't do it?" asked Will. His voice sounded funny, like he didn't dare say it.

"I don't think so."

"What's going to happen?" he asked.

"Maybe there's something I can do," I said.

CHAPTER TWENTY-EIGHT

I needed time to think and a quiet place to do it, so I headed for Sun Records. It was after six when I got there. The parking lot was empty. Elvis and the others must have finished recording.

I let myself in the back. Closing the door behind me, I turned around. Sam was sitting at the console, drinking a cup of coffee.

"So," he said, "back to do more cleaning?"

"I thought you had left. Where's your car?"

"It was acting up again. I took it to the filling station down the street."

He turned to the console, rewound a tape, and hit play. The voice of Elvis came floating from the speakers, singing the song they'd been working on, "Tomorrow Night." When it was done, Sam turned back to me.

"What do you think of that song?" he asked.

I shrugged. "It's fine."

Sam leaned forward, eyebrows dancing. "Come on, boy. You can do better than that."

"Well," I said, "it's kind of pretty. But it's not what Elvis does."

"What does Elvis do?"

"I can't describe it. I just feel it."

"What do you feel?" asked Sam.

It came out in a rush. "I feel like I don't belong. People act like everything's fine, but it's not. I feel bad. I feel angry. I feel like hitting someone."

"Do you feel like running away?" asked Sam.

"Running away? From what?"

"Home."

Sam knew. He had seen right through me. I tried to answer. I wanted to say that Sun Records was my home. I wanted to say a lot, but I found that I was crying. Sam watched me for a minute, then reached over and pulled up another chair. I sat down. I took a deep breath.

"I'm black," I said.

"How do you mean that?" he asked.

"I'm black. I'm Negro. Half, anyway."

I told him what my mother had said and what I'd learned from Will. I didn't leave anything out. When I finished, he shook his head.

"Well, what do you know."

"The only thing is," I said, "you have to keep it a secret."

He stared at me. "You're not going to tell anyone?"

"Will said not to. So did my mother."

Sam took a sip of coffee, then clasped his hands behind his head.

"You know," he said, "you remind me of some of the kids who come in here to play music. They usually have a song they've written. It's always bad. I tell them the same thing: Throw it away. Start over fresh. This time, look inside. Find something different, the one thing that nobody else has."

"Like Elvis did?"

"Lord, yes. Why do you think we spent so much time in the studio? We were searching. And we found it. I don't know what it is, or what to call it. But it's real. It lives and breathes. We let it out into the world. That's what we do at Sun Records."

Sam leaned forward. "Listen to me, Johnny. I know you better than you think. You're different. You're special. There's something wild inside of you. Don't cover it up. Don't deny it. Go with it. Hum it. Give it a tune. Move your lips. Move your body. You can do it, boy, I know you can."

"What if you're ashamed of it?" I said.

"Funny thing about that," said Sam. "Sometimes the things you're ashamed of turn out to be the most important. If you push them away, they come back. But if you grab hold of them, if you pull them to you and wrestle them to the ground, why, sometimes those are things you can use. They might even be beautiful."

"I don't know if I can do that."

"That's what they all say. I say it's hard work. It's the hardest work there is. But it's the best work."

I said, "I'll have to think about it."

"Now," said Sam, "I need you to do something for me."

"What's that?"

"Call your mother. She must be worried sick."

"I don't want to go back," I said.

"Son, I can't live your life for you. I'm just asking you to do what's right. After that, it's up to you."

She met me at the front door and hugged me so hard I thought I would burst. When she pulled away, her eyes were red, and her jaw was set in an angry line.

"Where have you been?" she demanded.

I told her about Sun Records and Nat D. and my conversation with Will. I tried to tell the truth. It wasn't pretty. It wasn't nice. But it was me.

She made supper, and while we ate she talked about Will and how they had met. She described mistakes she had made. She seemed to grow stronger as she talked.

Afterward we went for a walk. It was eight o'clock, and the sun was still up. The hot air was thick with moisture. The lawns were perfectly manicured. The houses were silent. Our neighborhood, home to the most powerful people in Memphis, looked beautiful and serene. I knew now that it was an illusion.

We walked down Belvedere Boulevard and turned onto Peabody Avenue. A few blocks down, there was a big house with pillars in front. It was the home of Boss Crump, the most powerful man in Memphis.

"He's in there, you know," said my mother, her voice low. "He's sick. He may not last out the year."

She said, "I met him one time. He came by the office to see Mr. Chapman. I'd always thought he would be big—you know, larger than life. He wasn't like that at all. He looked like somebody's grandfather. He was kind and polite, a real gentleman. You'd never know how powerful he was."

I gazed at the house. Maybe that's the way it was with power. The stronger it got, the less you could see it. If you had real power and planned things right, a well-placed word could get you just about anything you wanted.

We continued down the street. Somewhere in the distance, a mockingbird chattered.

"I went to see Lamont," I said. "He's innocent."

"Oh, Johnny."

"He didn't beat up Elvis. I know who did."

"You really believe that?"

"I'll tell you all about it. But I need to do something first."

"Is it really true?" she said. "You think he could get out of jail?"

"What's it worth to you?"

She gave me a funny look.

I said, "What price would you pay to get him out? Your job? Our house?"

She pursed her lips. Her eyes had a dark, hollow look. "What are you saying?"

"Would you really keep Lamont in jail so we can live like this?"

"It's not my decision," she said. "It's his."

"No, Mom, you're wrong. It's mine."

CHAPTER TWENTY-NINE

I stood in the office of Arthur Chapman, looking out the window at Front Street. It was Friday morning, and the National Cotton Company was already busy. The offices were bustling, and upstairs on the classing floor, Mr. Jack had already put in several hours' work.

I'd gotten a ride into town with my mother, who had dropped me off in front of the National Cotton building. When she went to park the car, I had slipped into the building and entered Mr. Chapman's empty office.

A long, black Continental came around the corner and parked in front of the building. Will got out. He opened the back door, and Mr. Chapman emerged, wearing a seer-sucker suit and straw hat. A minute later, I heard his footsteps in the hallway.

"Linda," he called to his secretary, "get Howell Wainwright on the phone."

When he entered the office, he hung his hat and coat on

the back of the door and turned toward his desk.

"Hello, sir," I said.

He looked at me, startled. "What are you doing here?"

"I'd like to talk."

"So would I. Not to you, though."

The phone buzzed. "I'll take this call," said Chapman, moving toward his desk. He said to me, "Don't ever come in here without permission."

"It's about Trey," I said.

Chapman paused. "Trey?"

"Last Saturday night."

He stared, as if he were trying to look through me. "Linda," he called, "tell Mr. Wainwright I'll phone back."

Chapman shut the door. He went to his desk, which was nearly as large as my whole room. Sitting down, he straightened a few items on the desktop and looked up at me.

"What about him?" he said.

I took a deep breath. My voice was shaking. "He beat up Elvis Presley. Then he forced Lamont Turner to confess to it."

Chapman listened, sitting perfectly still.

I said, "Trey told Lamont that Will had had an affair with a white woman. He said that if Lamont didn't go along, he would come to you. Will would lose his job, lose everything. He might even be lynched."

"That's absurd."

"Lamont was drunk. He'd been yelling at Elvis during a concert. He was the logical suspect, so the police arrested him. But Lamont didn't believe what Trey told him. He called Will from the station. When Will got there, Lamont asked him one question: Did you have an affair with a white woman?"

"And?"

"Will said yes. That's when Lamont knew Trey was telling the truth. So Lamont confessed. He told the police that he beat up Elvis Presley. But it wasn't true. He was just trying to save his father."

"Interesting theory."

I said, "It's not a theory. Trey did it."

Chapman said, "You have no idea what you're saying. First of all, Trey didn't do it. Second, even if he did, you don't want to touch this. Trust me."

I said, "Your son gave Will a choice that night, if you could call it that. I'll do the same for you."

An expression rippled across his face. On another man it might have been a smile. "You're going to give *me* a choice?"

I could feel my legs shaking. I thought of Elvis and the way his legs shook when he got nervous.

"Here's the choice," I said. "You can go to the police and tell them Lamont is innocent."

"Or?"

"Or I'll tell them myself. I might take Ruth Ann Morris with me."

"I don't like that one," said Chapman. "I don't like the other one either."

"If you're worried about Trey, I'm sure you can think of a way to get him out of it. You wouldn't even have to tell the police who did it. You could just say Lamont was doing a job for you when the crime happened. They'd believe you. You're Arthur Chapman."

"I see," he said.

He opened a desk drawer. Reaching in, he pulled something out. It was a nail file. He buffed the nails of his left hand, examining them in the morning light.

He said, "You're right about Trey, you know. He did it. Not that it matters. Lamont Turner will stay in jail. He'll be tried and will serve his time."

"I don't think so."

"You really believe this idea of yours is going to work, don't you?" said Chapman.

"Yes sir, I do."

"Unfortunately, you overlooked one thing. If you go to the police, you'll force my hand." He set down the nail file. "Tell me, Johnny, do you play poker?"

"Sometimes."

"Wonderful game. It reminds me of life. I'm good at both. You know what I've learned? You don't bet all your chips on one hand. You hold some back. When Trey spoke to Lamont Turner, he used just enough chips to win the bet. But we have more. If you play this hand, you're going to lose. I guarantee it. Fold, Johnny. I'm telling you as a friend."

"You're not my friend."

Chapman's expression hardened. "All right, then, I'll show you my hand. Here you go, Johnny. It's three spades."

"What do you mean?"

"Three spades. Will Turner. Lamont Turner. And you.

The white woman was your mother. Will Turner is your father. You're a Negro."

The room was still. Outside, cars drove back and forth on Front Street.

I said, "I know."

"You do? Who told you?"

"It doesn't matter," I said. Then I thought of something. "What about Trey? How did he find out?"

"He overheard me talking to Will last Friday in my office. It was right after I caught you and Will in the garage. Trey heard everything. When he got in trouble Saturday night, he decided to use some of the information. But not all of it. He told Lamont Turner that Will had had an affair with a white woman, but he didn't identify the woman, or her son. Those chips are just sitting there, waiting to be used."

"What are you going to do?" I asked.

"If you go to the police, I'll tell everybody you're a Negro. That's a promise."

I took a deep breath. My heart raced. "Go ahead. It's fine. It doesn't bother me."

He said, "You want to sit at the back of the bus? Use colored restrooms? I don't think so."

"I'm Will Turner's son. I'm not ashamed of it."

"What about the people you know?" he asked. "You think they'll still want to be your friends?"

"If they're really my friends, then yes."

He gazed at me for a moment. Then he pressed the button on his intercom. "Linda, send Mr. Jack down, please."

Chapman rose from his desk. Turning his back on me,

he went to the window. "Awful weather," he said. "Brutally hot."

A moment later, Mr. Jack came in. He closed the door behind him and strode over to the desk. "Yes, sir?"

Chapman said, "Johnny has something to tell you."

I looked up at Mr. Jack. His expression was simple, and his features were plain. Once he had told me that he was raised on a cotton farm in Mississippi, where Negro sharecroppers lived on the land. When he was my age, one of his jobs had been to take the sharecroppers their money each week. As he had told me about the conditions they lived in, there had been a look of revulsion on his face.

Chapman said, "Tell him, Johnny."

I tried to speak. No words came out.

"Go on," said Chapman.

I couldn't form the words.

"That'll be all, Mr. Jack," said Chapman.

Mr. Jack nodded. "See you, Johnny."

He headed for the door. When he did, I remembered what Nat D. had told me in another office just a few days before: There's too many secrets in the world. Set 'em free. Air 'em out.

As Mr. Jack opened the door, I said, "Wait. I have something to say."

He turned and faced me.

"My father is a Negro," I said. "He's Will Turner."

The room was silent. Things appeared to be just as they were a moment before, but everything had changed.

Mr. Jack's mouth tightened, and lines appeared around his eyes.

"Is that right," he said.

I could see him watching my face, noticing that my nose was broad and my lips were thicker than his. I was a different person, all because of a few words.

"I'll go now," he said. He closed the door behind him.

Chapman said, "Multiply that by a hundred. By a thousand."

I found myself blinking, thinking about the expression on Mr. Jack's face. I would remember it for a long time.

"The world is a cruel place," said Chapman. "Everybody tries to get ahead. They step on other people to do it. I step on Mr. Jack. Mr. Jack steps on you. There's more behind him. They're lining up, son. I'm not the one with a choice. You are. Are you going to be on the top or the bottom? Do you want to be a white man? Or a nigger?"

The word hit me like a punch. I thought of Will. I thought of Hattie Mae Johnson. The word had been a part of their lives. It was in the air all around them, like cotton dust, invisible most of the time but revealed every so often when the sun streamed through.

"I'm Will Turner's son," I said. "You can tell them whatever you want."

"You have no idea what you're doing," said Chapman.

I said, "If you want to keep Trey out of jail, here's what I'd like. Lamont goes free. Will stays at his job. So does my mother. We keep our house. Only one thing is different. We tell people that Will is my father."

"Oh, really?"

Chapman gazed at me for a long time. "So, that's your offer, is it?"

"Yes, sir."

"And if I don't agree?"

"Then I tell the police about Trey."

Chapman picked up the nail file again. He examined the nails on his other hand and buffed them lightly. "All right, then. Go ahead."

"I'm serious, sir. I'll do it."

"I believe you," he said.

"And you wouldn't try to stop me?"

"Why should I?"

I didn't understand. I studied his face, looking for clues.

He set down the nail file and folded his hands on the desk. "You're not too smart, are you, boy? I'm white. You're not. I'm Arthur Chapman. You're not. Whatever you do, I'll fix it. Whatever you soil, I'll clean it up. Now, get out of my office."

I said, "I'm going to get Lamont Turner out of jail."

"Good."

"You'll keep him on?" I asked.

"He may be impulsive, but he's a smart boy," said Chapman. "Did you know he's a mechanic? A good one, too. I can use him. Just like I can use your mother. And your father."

"You can't use me," I said.

"Maybe not now. But one of these days you'll change your mind. You'll need something, and you'll come to me. Or to Trey. We'll be waiting."

CHAPTER THIRTY

The heat wave broke the next day. That evening I sat with Will and Lamont on the front steps of Will's house, sipping iced tea and watching a pair of kids play next door.

After talking with Chapman, I had gone to see Trey. I told him I didn't care who knew about my father and said I was going to turn him in. After thinking it over, he decided to vouch for Lamont, on the condition that I keep him out of it. The police released Lamont, Trey got off free, and the mysterious beating of Elvis Presley faded away, along with the bruises on Elvis's face.

Next door, the kids squirted each other with a hose. The water glistened on their dark skin.

"They don't know what the world's like," said Lamont, gazing at the kids. "They got no idea."

"Is it really that bad?" I said. "They're just kids. They're people."

Lamont looked at me. "Man, you don't get it, do you?

We're Negroes. It's a white world, and we're black."

I looked at my hands. They were as white as ever.

"You had a chance," said Lamont. "Will gave it to you, but you gave it back. Now look at you. Sitting on a porch in the Negro part of town."

"I like it here. It's nice."

"You must be blind," said Lamont.

I thought of Sam Phillips. Maybe he was blind too. I had a feeling he didn't care. For Sam, the important thing wasn't seeing, but hearing. Listening. It was why he brought people out of the cotton fields to sing in a studio. It was how he noticed something different in the thin, uncertain voice of a white boy.

I said to Will, "Now I know why you wouldn't tell me about Carl Ross."

"Carl Ross never mattered," said Will. "He was just a cracker. He was a fool, leaving your mother."

I looked over at Will. There was something in his face I'd never seen before.

"Did you . . . love her?" I asked.

He swirled his iced tea and took a sip. "Still do."

I remembered the day my mother had told me that Will was trouble. I said, "Does she love you?"

"She did."

"You think you'll get together sometime?"

"No," he said.

"Why not?"

"Life's not like that."

"What if it could be?" I asked.

He shook his head. "Don't even ask the question."

Next door, a woman came out on the porch and called the kids. They turned off the water and went inside, giggling.

Behind us, a voice drifted through the screen door. It was Moohah Williams on WDIA. He cued a record, and Furry Lewis came on. He was playing the blues.

Three weeks later, a new shopping center opened at the corner of Lamar and Airways, out by the Rainbow Rollerdrome, where Elvis and Dixie had first met. The promoters wanted to draw a big crowd, so they made the opening into a major event. There were games and prizes, celebrity appearances, and a twenty-eight-foot wooden Indian. Musical groups performed on a flatbed truck in front of Katz Drug Store. The master of ceremonies was George Klein, a friend of Elvis's from Humes High who was a disc jockey on KOSE and was broadcasting the event live from inside the wooden Indian. Featured in all the ads was "the newest Memphis hit in the recording business, Elvis Presley."

I went to the opening that Thursday night. My mother asked if she could go with me, and I said yes. She and I had reached a stalemate. I had agreed to come home if she would let me keep working at Sun Records. We still weren't talking much, but it felt different around the house, as if someone had pulled up the shades and thrown open the windows. I was more comfortable there. Belvedere Boulevard hadn't changed. Maybe I had. It was the same as ever, silent and spotless and closed up tight. I didn't have all the answers, but I knew who I was and, when pressed, what I could do.

I didn't know if my mother would ever change. She still liked going to the Peabody Hotel, pretending she belonged. She continued to work with Chapman, staying on in the little house, accepting her salary with no complaints. A few times, though, I saw flashes of the woman who used to dance at the hotel. She and I talked more. Maybe she worried less. Once, when I played a blues record, she came to the kitchen doorway and stood there in her apron, listening. She nodded, smiling faintly, as if remembering the tune from a long time ago.

When we arrived at the shopping center, we found a big crowd, most of them between the ages of twelve and twenty. We met Elvis and Dixie by Katz Drugs.

"Are you excited?" I asked Elvis.

Elvis shrugged. "It's all right, I reckon."

"Don't let him fool you," said Dixie. "He's been talking about this for days."

Elvis had good reason to be happy. On August 18 his record had gone to number three on the country and western territorial charts, behind Hank Snow and Kitty Wells. On August 28 he had hit the regional charts in *Billboard* magazine. The following week, Bill Monroe himself had cut a new version of "Blue Moon of Kentucky" in 4/4 time, the way Elvis had sung it.

I was still working at Sun but had cut back to part-time when school started. One of the first things I had done after Lamont got out of jail was go to Sun, where Elvis was recording that day, and tell him that Will was my father and Lamont was my brother. Sam and I watched Elvis when I told him the news. His eyes opened wide.

"Lamont Turner's your brother?" he said. "Man, I knew there was something about you that I liked."

Sam said, "Elvis is jealous. You're what he's always dreamed of being—a white Negro."

They laughed at that. I laughed with them, relieved that it was all right.

At Katz Drugs, Scotty and Bill arrived. They went behind the flatbed truck with Elvis to get out their instruments and warm up. Dixie drifted off with some friends, and my mother and I went out front to get a good spot.

On the way, we saw Trey Chapman and Graydon Scarborough. Ruth Ann was with them. When Trey noticed me, he turned to the others and said something. Graydon laughed. Ruth Ann gazed at me for a moment, then started laughing too. She turned away, her glance flicking across me like a whip.

We bought some lemonade and found a place under a tree with a good view of the concert. A bagpipe band was just finishing up.

My mother looked over at me. "How are you feeling these days?"

"I'm fine."

"Are the kids picking on you?" she asked.

"Some of them. I guess I'm finding out who my friends are."

"You know, Johnny, we never talked about that day when you went to see Mr. Chapman. What did you tell him?"

"Nothing much."

"I think you're being modest," she said. "Lamont's out

of jail. I've still got my job. How did you do it?"

For some reason I didn't want to tell her what had happened—at least, not yet. I was still thinking about it.

"I just asked," I said.

She gazed at me for a moment, then leaned over and kissed me on the cheek.

The bagpipe band finished, and George Klein went to the microphone. "Okay, everybody, we have a real treat for you tonight. For the past two months, the number one record in Memphis has been something that was recorded right here in town. When I first heard it, I didn't know what to think. It sounded familiar, but it sounded different, too. One thing was for sure—I couldn't sit still.

"Imagine my surprise when I found out the record was by a classmate of mine from Humes High. He always said he was a singer, but we didn't believe him. Well, now we believe. You will, too. Please welcome my good friend, Elvis Presley!"

The crowd let out a sound that was different from anything I'd ever heard. It wasn't so much a cheer as an explosion, a wall of noise that burst across the parking lot like a sonic boom. People yelled and screamed and pushed, trying to get closer to the stage.

My mother and I stared at each other. Nothing—not the recording sessions, not Overton Park, not the Eagle's Nest—had prepared me for this.

Onstage, Elvis, Scotty, and Bill had started to play, but they were drowned out by the crowd. Girls screamed. Some of them looked like they were about to faint. Elvis, as surprised as anyone, started jumping around and shaking his legs. Bill slapped the bass, and Scotty grinned.

A long time ago, Lamont had told me there was nothing new in the world. He was wrong. New things do come along. Sometimes they're right beside you, and you don't even notice.

Something had happened in Memphis. No one quite knew what it was, but it was real. It was part country and part blues, part street and part gospel, part black and part white. Like me.

Then again, we're all black. We're all white. That's what Nat D. Williams says. That's what you learn on Beale Street, if you ask. And if you listen.

AUTHOR'S NOTE

America today is very different from America in 1950. It's urban. It's multiracial in ways that people back then could barely imagine. It's dominated by popular culture. It's constantly searching for things that are new and different, and then it discards them.

How did we get this way? What happened?

If you're looking for a starting point, I would suggest 1954, in Memphis, Tennessee. Old-time businesses, such as cotton companies, still thrived. Black and white people were rigidly segregated by race. And yet there were a few places where the races met, and many of those had to do with music.

One place was over the airwaves. Radio pioneers such as Nat D. Williams and Dewey Phillips played black music, primarily the blues, and white people listened. Some of those people found their way to clubs on Beale Street. One of them, a young man with acne and a shy grin, wandered into Sun Records, where, for a brief time, black and white musicians recorded side by side, listening to each other and learning.

The young man's name was Elvis Presley, and he soaked up music like a sponge—popular singers like Bing Crosby, blues musicians like B. B. King, black gospel performers like Queen C. Anderson, white gospel groups like the Statesmen, and country singers like Hank Williams and Bill Monroe. At Sun Records, he met Sam Phillips, a man in search of something new. Out of the bubbling stew that was Elvis Presley's musical life, that new thing emerged.

Some people say that Elvis copied the blues. Elvis himself probably would have admitted it. But the music that he and Sam Phillips created was more, and less, than black people had been singing for years. He didn't sound white, but in retrospect he didn't sound black either.

One thing is certain: Elvis Presley struck a chord. For those who were listening, he represented many things— mystery, intrigue, freedom, darkness, a driving beat, and just plain fun. They took him in and passed him around, examining every look and move. They made him a star and, ultimately, a freak.

In the beginning, though, he was a young man who lived for music, in a place that was ripe for change. I became fascinated by that place, initially through the writings of Peter Guralnick, Robert Gordon, and Stanley Booth. I wondered what it would be like to be a boy living there, searching for something. From that thought came Johnny Ross, who gave me a chance to walk down Beale Street with Elvis.

Johnny, his mother, Arthur Chapman, Trey Chapman, Graydon Scarborough, and Ruth Ann Morris are fictional. So are Will and Lamont Turner, as are many of the minor characters. But the events against which the fictional story is set were real. Some of the characters were also real, although they are used here in a fictional manner.

For example, in June of 1954 there was a cross-burning at Foote Homes very much like the one described in this novel. The year before, there was a bombing. There were in fact sessions at Sun Records with James Cotton and Pat Hare, the Starlite Wranglers, and Elvis Presley. The details of Elvis's sessions, first concerts, and early career are based on research as to what actually took place, although the verbal and physical attacks on Elvis at the Eagle's Nest are fictional.

In all my research, I found the historical characters I met, like Memphis itself, to be fascinating, varied, and outrageous—a wonderful and rich historical backdrop for this novel.

Elvis Presley, the shy young man from Tupelo, went on to become a show business legend, an American icon, and one of the most famous people who ever lived. Known as "The King," he had 112 Top Forty and 18 number one hits, sold over six hundred million singles and albums, starred in thirty-one motion pictures, and sold out Las Vegas showrooms. Though he died in 1977, to this day he has millions of fans. Some claim sightings and staunchly maintain that Elvis lives.

Sam Phillips worked with Elvis Presley until 1955, when he sold Elvis's contract to RCA Victor for $25,000, at that time the most ever paid for a recording artist. Phillips said he never regretted the sale, since it gave Elvis the national exposure he sought and provided Sun Records with the money needed to develop new talent. Over the next few years Phillips helped launch the careers of Johnny Cash, Roy Orbison, Jerry Lee Lewis, Carl Perkins, Charlie Rich, and dozens of others.

Marion Keisker, in addition to her important work at Sun Records, went on to help Sam Phillips start the first all-female radio station, WHER, in 1955. In 1957 she left Sun Records to join the Air Force, eventually reaching the rank of captain. She returned to civilian life in 1969 and spent the rest of her life in Memphis. Elvis said of Marion, "She's the one who made it all possible. Without her I wouldn't even be here."

Nat D. Williams continued his remarkable string of activities and accomplishments through the 1950s and 1960s. Besides his pioneering work on WDIA, his newspaper column, his role as host at the Palace Theater and other community events, and his forty-one-year teaching career at Booker T. Washington High School, he led a Boy Scout troop, taught Sunday school, and sang in the church choir, never missing a week in forty years. It was said that, for a time, he had more former students in state legislatures than any other African American teacher in the United States.

Dewey Phillips broadcast his groundbreaking radio program *Red Hot and Blue* until 1958. He had a brief try at television in 1956 as host of a dance show. In both radio and television, the wild, unpredictable behavior that made him so unique and popular led to his eventual downfall, and he was fired from both shows. Phillips never was able to recapture the magic of his glory days in the 1950s.

Scotty Moore, one of the most influential guitarists ever to play rock 'n' roll, stayed on with Elvis's band until 1957. He and Bill Black left the group over disagreements about money and billing, though they played with Elvis off and on during the years after that. Moore went on to produce and perform on recordings by many other artists and was co-owner and engineer at recording studios in Memphis and Nashville. The last time he played with Elvis was during the landmark "'68 Comeback" television special. Today Moore lives in Nashville.

Bill Black played with Elvis until 1957, when he went off on his own, forming the Bill Black Combo, which landed eight singles in the Top Forty between 1959 and 1962. The group appeared with the Beatles in 1964 during the British band's first American tour. Oddly, this pioneering group is rarely mentioned or heard of today.

James Cotton, after recording the classic "Cotton Crop Blues" at Sun Records in 1954, left Memphis and moved to Chicago to join the Muddy Waters Review. Forming his own band in 1967, he became popular with young people who sought the roots of rock 'n' roll, and he went on to win multiple Grammy awards. Cotton moved back to Memphis in 1994, where he lives and occasionally performs to this day.

Pat Hare also joined the Muddy Waters Review. When he left the band, he moved to Minneapolis and a short time later really did murder his girl-friend. Hare was sentenced to ninety-nine years in prison.

The Starlite Wranglers replaced Scotty Moore and Bill Black, but the band never was the same. Doug Poindexter tried the insurance business for a time and went on to own Southern Statistical Computer Consultants. For years Poindexter remained uncon-vinced about Elvis's talent, once saying, "Frankly, I thought the boy would starve to death."

Wynette Pugh, the girl who used to hang around rehearsals and sing with Elvis, later changed her name to Tammy Wynette. She wrote and recorded dozens of hit songs, including her trademark "Stand

By Your Man," winning Grammy awards and eventually becoming known as the "First Lady of Country Music."

Edward Hall "Boss" Crump built a political machine that dominated Memphis and the state of Tennessee for nearly fifty years. He died at his Peabody Avenue home on October 16, 1954.

Writing is thought to be a solitary activity, but as I worked on this story the room behind me was crowded with people who helped me along the way.

Some were writers. I read dozens of volumes, a handful of which were truly indispensable. *Last Train to Memphis: The Rise of Elvis Presley*, the first volume of Peter Guralnick's magnificent biography, brought Elvis to life. *Good Rockin' Tonight: Sun Records and the Birth of Rock 'n' Roll*, by Colin Escott with Martin Hawkins, painted a colorful, detailed portrait of Sam Phillips and Sun Records. *Wheelin' on Beale: How WDIA-Memphis Became the Nation's First All-Black Radio Station and Created the Sound that Changed America*, by Louis Cantor, introduced me to Nat D. Williams and WDIA. In *Beale Black & Blue: Life and Music on Black America's Main Street*, Margaret McKee and Fred Chisenhall took me by the hand and led me down Beale Street—not the tourist attraction of today but the living, breathing heart of Memphis's African American community before the street was decimated by urban renewal in 1969.

The gaps in my research were filled in graciously and

efficiently by John Dougan of the Shelby County Archives, Wayne Dowdy of the Memphis Public Library, and the staff of the Tennessee State Archives. Armed with a list of story locations and addresses, I drove to Memphis, where Fred James served as my able guide, sharing ice cream at the Dairy Queen and ribs at the Rendezvous. When the manuscript was finished, Scotty Moore was kind enough to read it and make some suggestions.

During the research, writing, and publication of the book I was helped and encouraged by my wonderful editors, Alyssa Eisner Henkin and Alexandra Cooper, and by my loyal agents, Jodi Reamer and Amy Berkower.

As always, at the heart of my writing are my wife, Yvonne Martin Kidd, and my daughter, Maggie. My parents, Paul and Ida Sue Kidd, encouraged and supported me, as did my brother, Russell Kidd, and my sister, Carol Sue Loscutoff. My good friend Tony Plog provided inspiration and the best example a writer could hope for.

And whenever I wrote, looming behind me, filling the room, stood Elvis Presley, the sad, shy, towering teenager who brought happiness to millions but couldn't seem to find it himself.